Good News for KIDS

52 GOSPEL TALKS

Series A

Elizabeth Friedrich
Shirley K. Morgenthaler
Eileen Ritter
Jane P. Wilke

CPH™
SAINT LOUIS

Copyright © 1995 Concordia Publishing House
3558 S. Jefferson Avenue, St. Louis, MO 63118-3968
Manufactured in the United States of America

Library of Congress Cataloging-in-Publication Data.

Good news for kids :   52 Gospel talks / Elizabeth Friedrich . . . [et al.].
  p.BP cm.
  Contents: [1] Series A
  ISBN 0-570-04823-0 (Series A)   :
  1. Bible—Liturgical lessons, English.   2. Christian education of children.   I.
Friedrich, Elizabeth, 1949– .
BS2565.G66   1995
252'.53—dc20   95-5762

1 2 3 4 5 6 7 8 9 10   04 03 02 01 00 99 98 97 96 95

Contents

————⟫◆⟪————

Be Ready—He's Coming Again

FIRST SUNDAY IN ADVENT: Matt. 24:37–44

Text: "Therefore keep watch, because you do not know on what day your Lord will come. ... So you also must be ready, because the Son of Man will come at an hour when you do not expect Him." *Matt. 24:42, 44*

Teaching aid: None

Gospel truth: Through faith in Jesus' death and resurrection for us, we wait expectantly for His return.

Have you ever spent the day at a baby-sitter's house or a day care center? Perhaps you have done this only a few times, or you may do it every day. Where did your parents go while you were at the sitter's? Why couldn't you go with them? *Allow the children to explain that they usually go to day care or have a sitter while their parents are working or busy.*

Think about what you do at the sitter's or the day care center while you are there. Do you just sit in a chair and wait for your parents to come back? Of course not! You might read a book or work a puzzle. You could play games with other children who are staying there. Maybe you would play out in the yard or ride bikes on the driveway. The sitter might take you to the library or the playground. If you go to the sitter's after school, you might start working on your homework.

Sometimes children worry at day care that their parents will never come back for them. They may not want to eat or rest or play. When their parents return, the children might be so upset that they cry even though they are happy to see them.

But you know that your parents will come back for you as soon as they are finished working. They promised they would come, and you know that they try to keep their promises because they love you. So you eat and play and rest and work while you are in day care. You may not be sure what time your parents will come, but you have faith that they will come for you at the right time.

Because of this faith, you will be ready when your parents come. You might be in the middle of doing something you really enjoy, but you will gladly put that activity away and go with your parents when they come for you. Although you like the sitter and what you do in day care, you know that your real home is with your parents, who love you most of all.

Jesus tells us in today's Gospel lesson that He will come again to take us to our home in heaven. While we live here on earth, we have many things to do. We enjoy some of them, like picnics and vacations and holidays. Some times are not so happy, like times when we are sick or when someone we love dies. Then we are glad to have the family and friends Jesus has given us here on earth.

But we know that Jesus will come to take us to heaven, just as He promised. We will be ready to go with Him because He made us ready by dying on the cross to take our sins away. We won't feel sad to leave what we are doing here because we know that our real home is in heaven with Jesus, the one who loves us most of all.

Prayer: Dear Lord Jesus, we know from Your Word that You are coming again. Forgive our sins and keep our faith strong so that we will be ready to meet You and will look forward to Your coming with joy. In Your name we pray. Amen.

Repent
and Be Ready

———◆———

SECOND SUNDAY IN ADVENT: Matt. 3:1–12

Text: In those days John the Baptist came, preaching in the Desert of Judea and saying, "Repent, for the kingdom of heaven is near." *Matt. 3:1–2*

Teaching aids: Two note cards. One card reads, "I'm coming to visit you for Christmas. Love, Cousin Tom." The other note card is blank.

Gospel truth: Our sin stands in the way of our relationship with God; but He forgives us for Jesus' sake and helps us live lives that are pleasing to Him.

Wouldn't it be fun to have company for Christmas? Grandparents, aunts, and uncles really add to our enjoyment of the holiday. And if you have cousins who are about your age, you would really look forward to having them come to visit you at Christmas.

You would probably be excited to get a letter like this in the mail. *Read the message on the first note card.* Let's pretend you visited cousin Tom last summer when you were on your vacation. You had lots of fun playing together at his house. You enjoyed seeing his school and neighborhood and meeting his friends.

Now Tom is coming to visit you for Christmas. You start to plan the fun things you will do together and the places you will take him. You get out a piece of paper to write him a letter about all the fun you're going to have.

But as you think about your visit to Tom's house, you remember what happened the day before you left. While

Tom was away taking his piano lesson, you borrowed his bike, even though he had asked you not to ride it. You rode around the block a few times, then left the bike lying in the driveway. When Aunt Ellen backed out the car to pick up Tom, she didn't see the bike, and she ran over it with her car. You were afraid when you saw how angry Tom was about the bike. So you said you had been playing video games while Tom was at his lesson and that one of the neighbors must have used his bike and left it in the driveway. You didn't ever want Tom to know what you had done.

Now all you can think about is Tom's twisted bike. When you try to write to Tom, you see his sad face when he found his broken bike. The wrong thing that you did and the lie you told stand like a wall between you and Tom.

How can you get rid of that wall of sin so that you will be able to have fun with Tom again? *Show the children the blank note card and let them suggest writing to Tom, telling him truthfully what they had done and asking his forgiveness.*

When Jesus was ready to begin His ministry on earth, God sent John the Baptist with a message for the people. John said, "Repent, for the kingdom of heaven is near." He told people to repent—to tell God about the wrong things they had done that stood in the way of their relationship with God. He told them to be sorry for their sins so that they could be glad to see Jesus, whom God had promised to send to be their Savior.

Jesus took the punishment for our sins when He died on the cross. God forgives us for Jesus' sake. He takes the wall of sin away and we are happy to live as His children again. Listen for the words *repent* and *heaven* in church today.

Prayer: God, thank You for sending Your Son, Jesus, to die for our sins. Forgive us for His sake and bless our happy relationship with You. In Jesus' name we pray. Amen.

Jesus—The Perfect Man for the Job

⟹◆⟸

THIRD SUNDAY IN ADVENT: Matt. 11:2–11

Text: Jesus replied, "Go back and report to John what you hear and see: The blind receive sight, the lame walk, those who have leprosy are cured, the deaf hear, the dead are raised, and the good news is preached to the poor." *Matt. 11:4–5*

Teaching aids: Three sheets of poster board on which you have written the job descriptions described in the talk.

Gospel truth: Jesus came in fulfillment of the Old Testament prophecies to be God in action among His people—healing, restoring, and ultimately redeeming us through His death on the cross.

When businesses or organizations plan to hire a new employee, they often write a job description telling what they expect this employee to do. I've brought along some job descriptions this morning. Can you tell me what kind of worker this job description tells about?

Read the first description. "Be in the classroom from 8 a.m. to 4 p.m. Prepare daily lesson plans for all subjects. Help students individually. Supervise playground and lunchroom when it's your turn. Evaluate students' work on report cards every nine weeks."

Give the children time to answer. Yes, this job description tells what a teacher does. Let's try another one.

Read the second description. "Lead the congregation's worship service and preach a sermon about God's Word.

Provide Baptism and the Lord's Supper. Visit the sick and help those with problems. Serve at weddings and funeral services. Teach God's Word to children and adults."

Give the children time to answer. That's right, this job description tells about the work of a pastor.

Before Jesus began His ministry, John the Baptist called people to repent—to tell God they were sorry for their sins. He told them that the kingdom of heaven was near. The people who heard John knew that the Messiah God had promised was coming. If they, like John, had read the prophecies of Isaiah, they knew that this Messiah would save them from their sins.

Isaiah's job description for the Messiah looked something like this. *Display the third job description.* "He will make the blind to see, the deaf to hear, and the lame to leap like a deer. He will preach good news to the poor. He will save His faithful people" (Is.29:18–21; 35:4–7; 42:1–16; 61:1–3).

After John had baptized Jesus, he was thrown into prison by King Herod. While in prison, he heard about Jesus' preaching and the miracles He was performing. He wanted to know for sure that Jesus was the Messiah. So John sent his disciples to find out.

When John's disciples asked Jesus if He was the one God had promised, Jesus answered, "Go back and report to John what you hear and see: The blind receive sight, the lame walk, those who have leprosy are cured, the deaf hear, the dead are raised, and the good news is preached to the poor." Jesus fit Isaiah's job description perfectly.

All that Jesus did showed God's mercy—that He had come to help people in their trouble. He fulfilled Isaiah's prophecy completely when He died on the cross to save all people from their worst trouble—sin.

Prayer: Dear Lord Jesus, we're so glad you came, just as the prophets said You would. Thank You for showing us God's mercy by helping us in all of our troubles, especially our greatest trouble—sin. In Your name we pray. Amen.

What's in a Name?

———◆———

FOURTH SUNDAY IN ADVENT: Matt. 1:18–25

Text: "She will give birth to a son, and you are to give Him the name Jesus, because He will save His people from their sins."

All this took place to fulfill what the Lord had said through the prophet: "The virgin will be with child and will give birth to a son, and they will call Him Immanuel"—which means, "God with us." *Matt. 1:21–23*

Teaching aids: A book of names and their meanings; two large poster-board cards that say, "*Jesus* = He will save His people from their sins" and "*Immanuel* = God with us."

Gospel truth: Jesus, the Son of God, came to be with us as true God and true man to save us from our sins.

Parents getting ready for the birth of a baby have lots of decisions to make. One of these decisions is what to name the new baby. Will they name it after one of their relatives, or will they choose a name they like in a movie or television show or in the Bible?

When your parents were expecting you, they may have used a book like this to find a name that would be right for you. The name that they chose has a meaning. This meaning might tell about you and your personality. Or the meaning of the name might not fit you at all.

For example, my first name is _____. This name means _____. *Look up your name in the book. Then tell why you think your name does or doesn't fit you.*

Let's see what some of your names mean. *Look up the names of two or three children and read the meanings.*

Our Gospel lesson today tells about the most important birth that ever took place. Mary and Joseph were expecting a baby. Joseph was worried because he and Mary were not married yet, and he knew that he was not the baby's father. Because of this, according to Jewish law, Joseph would have to break his engagement to Mary. Otherwise Mary could be punished, even killed, for having a baby before she was married.

One night an angel from God came to Joseph in a dream. He told Joseph not to be afraid to marry Mary. He said that Mary's baby came from God and that God Himself was the baby's Father.

Then the angel told Joseph what he and Mary should name the baby. *Show the first card.* "You are to give Him the name Jesus," said the angel, "because He will save His people from their sins."

When Jesus lived on earth, He obeyed His heavenly Father perfectly in our place. And in our place He suffered and died on the cross to pay for our sins. His name, Jesus, describes exactly who He is and what He did.

The prophet Isaiah used another name for Jesus: *Immanuel*, which means "God with us." *Show the second card.* Mary and Joseph must have thought about this name, Immanuel, as they looked at their special baby. By becoming a human baby, God was really with His people.

Jesus, our Savior, is still our Immanuel today. He is with us so that we never need to feel afraid. And He will someday take us home to be forever with Him in heaven.

Prayer: Lord Jesus, we know You came to save us from our sins. We ask You to forgive us for all the things we have done wrong. Be our Immanuel—God with us—everywhere we go and in everything we do. In Your name we pray. Amen.

The Cross in the Manger

FIRST SUNDAY AFTER CHRISTMAS:
Matt. 2:13–15, 19–23

Text: When they had gone, an angel of the Lord appeared to Joseph in a dream. "Get up," he said, "take the child and His mother and escape to Egypt. Stay there until I tell you, for Herod is going to search for the child to kill Him." *Matt. 2:13*

Teaching aids: Draw a simple picture of Baby Jesus in the manger. Decorate with markers or crayons. Draw the outline of a cross on the back of the picture. Or draw the cross on the back of a Christmas picture from a Sunday school leaflet. Have scissors available.

Gospel truth: God sent His Son, Jesus, to be born as a human being so that He could die in our place to take away our sins.

I love Christmas—the music, the decorations, the food, the presents! Most of all, I love to read the story of the first Christmas from the Bible. *Display the manger picture.* This picture reminds me of that story. Can you tell me what happened? *Allow time for the children to retell the story of Jesus' birth.*

What a beautiful story! Everybody loves the story about the new baby, and His mother and father, and the angels and shepherds, the Wise Men and the star.

But in today's Gospel lesson, we hear something that doesn't seem to belong to the beautiful Christmas story. As soon as the Wise Men had left Bethlehem to go back to their own country, an angel appeared to Joseph in a dream. "Take the child and His mother and go to Egypt," the angel said. "King Herod is going to look for Jesus so he can kill Him."

Kill Him? This doesn't seem to fit the Christmas story at all. Why would anyone want to hurt that cute little baby in the manger?

But King Herod didn't think of Jesus as a cute little baby. When the Wise Men told him they were looking for the king of the Jews, Herod became jealous. After all, he was the king of the Jews, and thinking about someone else living in his palace and wearing his crown made him angry. The more angry he became, the more he hated the baby the Wise Men had come to worship. In anger King Herod devised a plan. He sent his soldiers to Bethlehem to kill all the baby boys who lived there. Then he wouldn't have to worry about this king of the Jews.

Jealousy, anger, hatred, murder. King Herod's sins ruin the beautiful picture of Christmas. *Following the cross you outlined on the back, cut along both lines of one side of the horizontal arm into the center.* Sin spoils everything beautiful that God gave us. *Cut along the lines on the other side of the horizontal arm into the center.* Maybe our sins even spoiled the beautiful Christmas celebrations we had planned with our families. Maybe we want more and better presents than we received. Maybe we fought with our brothers and sisters or disobeyed our parents. *Cut along the lines of the bottom of the vertical part of the cross into the center.*

But the manger and the baby were only the beginning of God's plan. *Cut out the rest of the cross.* There in the manger was God's answer for sin. *Display the cross.* Because of God's great love for us, Jesus would grow up and live a perfect life in our place. He would teach and heal and show people what God's love is like. Then He would die on a cross to pay for all the terrible things we have done and rise again to win us new life.

King Herod's story reminds us of the reason for Christmas—God sent His Son to save us from our sin.

Prayer: Dear Heavenly Father, our sin, like Herod's, has spoiled our Christmas celebration. Forgive us, for the sake of Jesus, who was born in the manger and died on the cross for us. In Jesus' name we pray. Amen.

Now Appearing in Person— God, Himself

SECOND SUNDAY AFTER CHRISTMAS:
John 1:1–18

Text: In the beginning was the Word, and the Word was with God, and the Word was God. ... The Word became flesh and made His dwelling among us. We have seen His glory, the glory of the One and Only, who came from the Father, full of grace and truth. ... No one has ever seen God, but God the One and Only, who is at the Father's side, has made Him known. *John 1:1, 14, 18*

Teaching aid: A picture of Jesus.

Gospel truth: Jesus, who is true God, took on human form to live, suffer, and die in our place for our sins. Only in Jesus can we know what God is like.

How would you describe God? Without talking about Jesus, can you tell me what God is like? *Allow time for the children to answer. They may mention creation or God's power as shown in natural events, but this will be a difficult question for young children.*

People have always had trouble describing God. He does such powerful things, causing the wind to blow and the waves to roll against the rocks. We know He made everything that exists, from lightning to lightning bugs, from mountains to flowers. But how can you talk to someone whose voice is mightier than the thunder?

Long ago God talked to His people, the children of Israel. He called them together at a mountain named Sinai. God came to the people in a thick cloud on the mountain. The people heard God's voice in the sound of thunder. They saw fire and smoke on top of the mountain, and they felt the mountain shake. They were scared to death.

But God didn't want His people to know only His power. He wanted to save them from their worst trouble—sin. So He sent Jesus to earth as a human being. *Show the picture of Jesus.* Jesus was like us in every way, except that He didn't sin. Because He was human, He knew how it felt to be hungry or tired or cold. He even knew what it was like to be tempted as we are.

Because Jesus was God and was also human like us, we know what God is like. Jesus was perfect, just as God is perfect. Jesus cared about people and showed He cared by listening to them and healing them when they were sick or crippled. Jesus explained what God is like and how He wants us to live using everyday examples like fig trees, shepherds and their sheep, fathers and their children.

Most of all, we see God in what Jesus did when He died on the cross for us. He took upon Himself all the sins of all the people who ever lived. He died on the cross as the punishment for those sins. Then He came alive again. Now when God looks at us, He doesn't see our sins—He only sees what Jesus did for us.

Jesus promised He would always be with us. We can't see Him now because He is no longer with us as a human being. But we know, as we know that He died for us and rose again, that He will keep His promise to be with us always.

Prayer: Dear Jesus, we needed help for the lives we messed up by our sin. Thank You for becoming a human being to share our lives here on earth. We especially thank You for taking our sins and dying for them on the cross. In Your name we pray. Amen.

Three Wise Kings

THE EPIPHANY OF OUR LORD: Matt. 2:1–12

Text: When they saw the star, they were overjoyed. On coming to the house, they saw the child with His mother Mary, and they bowed down and worshiped Him. Then they opened their treasures and presented Him with gifts of gold and of incense and of myrrh. *Matt. 2:10–11*

Teaching aids: A paper crown for each child, decorated with stick-on stars or "jewels." (One of the major fast-food chains will usually give you a supply of these for the asking.)

Gospel truth: Jesus came to earth to save us from our sins. God's Holy Spirit helps us respond with joyful obedience, worship, and stewardship.

Who do you think would wear a crown like this? *Place a crown on your own head.*

Yes, crowns are usually worn by kings and queens. In some countries, a king or queen is the head of the government. A good king or queen makes wise decisions to rule his or her people well.

Today's Gospel lesson tells about some Wise Men from the east who came to visit Baby Jesus. They had spent their lives studying the stars. When they saw a new star in the sky that meant a new king had been born, they left their home and followed that star to find the king. We sometimes call the Magi "kings" because the three gifts they brought to Jesus were very expensive—the kind kings would bring each other.

Because the Wise Men were looking for a king, they went first to Jerusalem, to the palace of King Herod. "Where's the one who has been born king of the Jews?" they asked. But no one at the palace knew anything about a newborn king.

King Herod asked his priests and teachers if they knew where the King God had promised would be born. "In Bethlehem," they answered. "That's what the prophets wrote."

When the Wise Men left Herod's palace, they saw the star again. With great joy they followed the star to Bethlehem, to the house where Jesus, Mary, and Joseph were staying. They worshiped Jesus as their King and gave Him fine gifts: gold, incense, and myrrh.

As we look at the story of the Wise Men, God's Holy Spirit teaches us how to love and worship Jesus. The Wise Men knew that Jesus was the King who had been promised to them. We, too, believe in Jesus and know that He was sent to be our Savior. *Place crowns on the heads of a few children.*

How happy the Wise Men must have been when they followed the star to Bethlehem and found Baby Jesus. God's Holy Spirit helps us follow Jesus with joy, rather than grumbling about obeying Him. *Place crowns on a few more children.*

The Wise Men worshiped Jesus. We, too, worship Jesus in church, in Sunday school, and in family devotions. *Crown a few more heads.*

And the Wise Men brought treasures to Jesus. We do the same when we bring our offerings to Sunday school and church and when we give our love to Jesus. *Make sure all the children have crowns.*

Listen for the words *Wise Men* and *star* during church today, and thank God for letting the Wise Men be our example in worshiping Jesus.

Prayer: Lord Jesus, we know You are our King. You died to take all our sins away. Help us joyfully obey, worship, and serve You with our gifts. In Your name we pray. Amen.

I'm Baptized—
Just Like Jesus!

THE BAPTISM OF OUR LORD: Matt. 3:13–17

Text: Then Jesus came from Galilee to the Jordan to be baptized by John. … As soon as Jesus was baptized, He went up out of the water. At that moment heaven was opened, and He saw the Spirit of God descending like a dove and lighting on Him. And a voice from heaven said, "This is my Son, whom I love; with Him I am well pleased." *Matt. 3:13, 16–17*

Teaching aids: A doll and a dish of water (*or use the baptismal font*).

Gospel truth: Through Baptism, we share in the righteousness Jesus won for us through His death and resurrection and become God's beloved children.

John the Baptist preached in the desert and called people to repent and be baptized for their sins. How surprised John must have been one day to see his cousin Jesus standing before him, waiting to be baptized. John believed that Jesus was the Savior God had promised. He had spent his life telling people that Jesus was coming. "I need to be baptized by You," John said to Jesus. "Why do You come to me?"

But Jesus answered, "It's right to do this to fulfill all righteousness." Even though Jesus never sinned, He did all that is required for us sinners.

After Jesus was baptized, John saw a dove come down from heaven and rest on Jesus. This bird was really the Holy

Spirit. Then God the Father's voice from heaven said, "This is My Son, whom I love and with whom I am well pleased."

Have you seen people baptized here in church? Maybe you were baptized here. If you were baptized as a baby, your parents and sponsors carried you to the baptismal font because you couldn't walk by yourself. You couldn't answer the pastor's questions. You couldn't even understand what was happening to you.

The pastor made the sign of the cross on your head and heart. He asked you if you believed in God, the Father, Son, and Holy Spirit. Your sponsors answered, "Yes." Then the pastor poured water on your head. He said, "I baptize you in the name of the Father, Son, and Holy Spirit." *Demonstrate with the doll and the water.*

Just as the Holy Spirit came to Jesus in the shape of the dove, He came to you when you were baptized. He put faith in Jesus in your heart. As you grow older, He helps your faith grow. He gives you teachers at church and Sunday school to help you learn more about Jesus and what He did for you. He helps you live the way Jesus wants you to live.

Through Baptism, you became God's beloved child, just like Jesus. Through Baptism, you share all that Jesus did— His perfect life, His death on the cross, and His rising from the dead. When God looks at you, He doesn't see your sin anymore—He sees Jesus' goodness and love. And He is well-pleased.

When you are worried about wrong things you have done, remember your Baptism. Ask God to forgive you. After all, you are His baptized child, and—because of Jesus—He will forgive you. Listen for the word *baptized* in church today.

Prayer: Dear God, we know that we have done many things wrong, and we don't deserve to be Your children. But You have made us Yours through Baptism. Through Baptism, we have died and risen with Jesus. Forgive our sins for His sake. In Jesus' name we pray. Amen.

He Brought His Brother

——⟫◆⟪——

SECOND SUNDAY AFTER THE EPIPHANY:
John 1:29–41

Text: Andrew, Simon Peter's brother, was one of the two who heard what John had said and who had followed Jesus. The first thing Andrew did was to find his brother Simon and tell him, "We have found the Messiah" (that is, the Christ). And he brought him to Jesus. *John 1:40–42a*

Teaching aid: A basketball.

Gospel truth: Called to faith in Jesus, our Savior from sin, we share the Good News with our family and friends.

Let me tell you a story about a boy named Andy, who loved sports. When we were in junior high, Andy wanted to play basketball more than anything else in the world. *Dribble or toss the basketball occasionally as you speak.* He shot hoops in his driveway before school every morning. He hung around the school playground until suppertime, hoping for a pick-up game with some of the other kids.

One day Andy discovered a boys' club in the town where we lived. After school he rode his bike to the club and followed the sound of dribbling balls to the gym.

The coach spotted Andy waiting shyly in the corner. "Want to play, kid?" he asked. Andy joined the three-on-three game at one end of the gym. By suppertime the coach had invited Andy to play on one of the club teams and had even given him his own uniform.

Andy rode home for supper too excited to even think

about eating. "Pete! Pete!" he called to his brother. "You've got to come with me tomorrow. I made the basketball team at the boys' club, and you could be on it too!"

The next afternoon Pete went with Andy to the gym. He joined the boys playing three-on-three. And the coach invited him to join the team and gave him a uniform too.

Pete and Andy played basketball together at the club all through junior high. Then something funny happened. Andy stopped growing at 5'10". He still loved to play basketball, and he made the high school team, but he didn't usually get to play until his team was far ahead. He was too short to play ball in college. Pete, however, kept right on growing. By tenth grade he was almost 6'5". He led his high school team to the state championship, was named a college All-American, and even went on to play in the NBA.

Andy never made as many baskets as his brother Pete. He never made the all-state squad or played in the NBA. But he did one very important thing for basketball—he brought his brother Pete.

In our Gospel lesson today, Matthew tells us about Andrew, who had been a follower of John the Baptist. When John pointed out Jesus as the Lamb of God, Andrew followed Him. Andrew believed that Jesus was the promised Savior.

Andrew was so excited to find the Savior that he went home and told his brother, Simon Peter. He brought Peter to Jesus. Andrew never wrote a book in the Bible. He's only mentioned a few more times in the New Testament. But his brother Peter, whom he brought, became a leader among the disciples and in the early church. God's Holy Spirit brought thousands of people to Jesus through Peter's work.

Like Andrew, we have found Jesus, the Savior. Like Andrew, we can share that Good News with our family and friends.

Prayer: Dear Lord Jesus, we know that You are the one God sent to die on the cross for our sins. Help us tell the people we know that You are their Savior too. We pray in Your holy name. Amen.

Following the Leader

———≫◆≪———

THIRD SUNDAY AFTER THE EPIPHANY:
Matt. 4:12–23

Text: As Jesus was walking beside the Sea of Galilee, He
saw two brothers, Simon called Peter and his brother
Andrew. They were casting a net into the lake, for they
were fishermen. "Come, follow Me," Jesus said, "and I
will make you fishers of men." At once they left their
nets and followed Him. *Matt. 4:18–20*

Teaching aid: None.

Gospel truth: Jesus calls us to leave everything and follow
Him.

Jenny couldn't wait to join Brownies. She remembered
how much fun her sister Sara had when she was a Brownie.
She had even learned the Brownie promise and tried on
Sara's old uniform.

But when Jenny turned seven years old, she didn't know
which Brownie troop she should join. She wanted to be sure
the troop had a good leader so the girls would be able to do
lots of fun activities. But she didn't know how to choose
which leader would be best for her.

Then one day Mrs. Vasquez called Jenny on the phone.
"I'm the leader of the Brownie troop at Stone School," Mrs.
Vasquez said. "I'd like to invite you to Brownies tomorrow."

Jenny was glad Mrs. Vasquez wanted her to be in her
troop and had called to invite her. "I didn't know where to go
until Mrs. Vasquez called me," said Jenny. "I'll join her troop
because she chose me."

In today's Gospel lesson, Matthew tells how Jesus called four of His disciples. Jesus saw Peter and Andrew fishing on the Sea of Galilee. He called out to them, "Come, follow Me, and I will make you fishers of men." Later He saw James and John getting ready to fish. He called James and John to follow Him.

Peter, Andrew, James, and John knew there was something special about a leader who came and asked them to follow Him. They left their nets, boats, and families and followed Jesus.

In our Baptism, Jesus calls each of us to follow Him. With His help, we leave behind the things that seem important to us—having our own way, doing what we want to do, being the most popular kid in the class or on the playground. We repent—tell Jesus we're sorry for the wrong things we have done. We follow Jesus because He has chosen us and gave His life for us.

Peter, Andrew, James, and John followed Jesus all over Galilee, heard Him preach on hillsides, and saw Him heal people who were sick or crippled, blind or deaf. They followed Him to Bethany and watched Him raise Lazarus from his grave. They followed Him to Gethsemane where He prayed. John even followed Him to Calvary and saw Him die on the cross.

Jesus calls us to follow Him all the way to Calvary, where He died to pay for our sins. We know that we deserve the punishment He took. But through faith we stand before God in the forgiveness He won for us.

We follow Jesus to the Easter garden, singing alleluias because He rose from the dead, and to the mountain where He ascended back into heaven. And we know that one day we will follow Him there, also, to live with Him forever.

Prayer: Dear Lord Jesus, You have called us to follow You. Forgive us for the sins that nailed You to the cross. Keep us as Your followers until we meet You in heaven. In Your name we pray. Amen.

Just the Opposite

FOURTH SUNDAY AFTER THE EPIPHANY: Matt. 5:1–12

Text: "Blessed are the poor in spirit, for theirs is the kingdom of heaven. Blessed are those who mourn, for they will be comforted. Blessed are the meek, for they will inherit the earth." *Matt. 5:3–5*

Teaching aids: Three pieces of poster board on which you have printed the following pairs of opposites, one on each side of the paper: rich and proud—poor in spirit; laugh—mourn; bold—meek.

Gospel truth: Through His grace, Jesus gives repentant sinners who come to Him in faith the gifts of His forgiveness, righteousness, and true joy.

Let's play a game of opposites. I'll give you a word, and you tell me its opposite. Hot. *Give the children time to respond.* Yes, cold is the opposite of hot. Let's try another—little. *Continue until you have established that the children understand the concept of opposites.*

Jesus taught His disciples a lesson in opposites. He wanted to show them what it would be like to follow Him. I've written some of the pairs of words He used on these cards.

Show the "rich and proud" side of the first card. Ask one of the children to read the words. What is the opposite of rich and proud? *Allow time for a response; then flip the card over.* Rich sounds good to us, but poor isn't something we would like to be. Jesus said, "Blessed are the poor in spirit, for theirs is the kingdom of heaven." People who are poor in spirit know that they haven't lived the way God said to live. They know they are sinners and need God's forgiveness.

Let's try another card. *Show the "laugh" side of the second card.* We like to laugh, and we would rather be happy all the time than have to feel sad about anything. *Flip the card.* But Jesus said, "Blessed are those who mourn, for they will be comforted." *Mourning* means feeling sad and sorry. We feel sorry for the things we have done wrong. Our sins make us sad. Jesus tells us that He alone comforts sinners and takes that sadness away.

Read the third card for me. *Display the "bold" side of the card.* A person who is bold is not afraid to talk to or work with other people. *Flip the card.* But a person who is meek thinks he isn't good enough to work with others or have what other people have. Jesus said, "Blessed are the meek, for they will inherit the earth." He was talking about being meek with God. Because we are sinners, we know that we don't deserve God's love or any of the good things He gives us. But because Jesus died for us, He promises to give us all good things.

"Blessed," Jesus said. Listen for the word *blessed* in church today. *Blessed* means much more than *happy*, which is a feeling that can go away as soon as sad things happen. *Blessed* means full of the joy that God gives—the joy that comes from knowing that Jesus has forgiven our sins and that we belong to Him forever.

Prayer: Dear God, our sins make us poor in spirit. We come to You meekly, sorry for all we have done wrong. Forgive us because Your Son, Jesus, died to make us righteous and holy in Your sight. In Jesus' name we pray. Amen.

Light for the World

—————◆—————

FIFTH SUNDAY AFTER THE EPIPHANY:
Matt. 5:13–20

Text: "You are the light of the world. A city on a hill cannot be hidden. Neither do people light a lamp and put it under a bowl. Instead they put it on its stand, and it gives light to everyone in the house. In the same way, let your light shine before men, that they may see your good deeds and praise your Father in heaven." *Matt. 5:14–16*

Teaching aids: One candle, matches, an opaque glass mixing bowl, a candlestick (preferably a tall one), and as many mirrors as you can find (all different sizes).

Gospel truth: Jesus, the Light of the world, calls His redeemed followers to reflect His life-giving light to others.

Who can tell me why we need light? *Encourage the children to explore the reasons, including to help us see where we're going or what we're doing, to help us find things, to keep us from falling over things we can't see.*

Jesus said, "I am the light of the world. Whoever follows Me will never walk in darkness, but will have the light of life" (John 8:12). Jesus explained that people love darkness when they sin because others will not be able to see the bad things they do. He said that those who follow Him and believe in Him as their Savior live in His light, so everyone will be able to see what God has done through them.

Light the candle. In today's Gospel lesson, Jesus told His disciples, "You are the light of the world. A city on a hill cannot be hidden." Jesus wanted them to know that they, as His followers, shared His light. They would be noticed, just as people always see a brightly lit town on a hilltop. Their light would seem especially bright to sinners still lost in darkness without Jesus.

Jesus warned the disciples not to hide their lights under a bowl where no one would be able to see it. *Hold the bowl over the candle.* A hidden light adds no light at all to the room. Instead, Jesus said we should put the light on a stand so it can give light to everyone in the house. *Place the candle in the candlestick.*

Jesus tells each of us, "You are the light of the world." My candle is like Jesus, the one true Light. These mirrors will help you see how you can be a light too. *Distribute the mirrors among the children.* Hold your mirror so the shiny side is pointed at my candle. What do you see in your mirror? What do you see in the mirrors around you? *The children should be able to see the candle reflected in each of the mirrors. Adjust the mirrors as needed.*

I'm still holding the only candle. But I can see candlelight in every mirror. Instead of one light, we now have many lights. We didn't buy more candles. The mirrors reflect the light of the only candle. Big mirrors, little mirrors, round mirrors, square mirrors—all reflect the candle's light.

The light that people see in you doesn't come from you, but it's a reflection of the light that is Jesus. We reflect Jesus' light when we love one another, when we are kind and patient and forgiving like He is, when we pray for each other, and when we help those around us. People also see Jesus' light in us when we tell them how He died for us and that He died to be their Savior from sin too. When I look at your mirror, I see a reflection of the candle. When I look at you—a child redeemed by Jesus' blood—I see a reflection of Jesus.

Prayer: Lord Jesus, we praise You for dying to take away our sins and make us Your children. Make us lights to everyone around us, that we may reflect Your love and that they may see You as their Savior too. In Your name we pray. Amen.

Holy—or Just Full of Holes?

———⟫◈⟪———

SIXTH SUNDAY AFTER THE EPIPHANY: Matt. 5:20–37

Text: "For I tell you that unless your righteousness surpasses that of the Pharisees and the teachers of the law, you will certainly not enter the kingdom of heaven. You have heard that it was said to the people long ago, 'Do not murder, and anyone who murders will be subject to judgment.' But I tell you that anyone who is angry with his brother will be subject to judgment." *Matt. 5:20–22a*

Teaching aids: A paper bag into which you have placed a dirty, torn shirt.

Gospel truth: When we rely on keeping the Law for our salvation, we clothe ourselves in the filthy rags of our own unrighteousness. But Christ, through His death in our place, gives us the perfect garment of His righteousness.

In today's Gospel lesson, Jesus teaches His disciples what it means to be righteous. *Righteous* means "perfect and holy, having obeyed all of God's rules completely."

The Pharisees and teachers of the law knew the importance of being righteous. They prided themselves on how hard they worked to keep every word of God's Law exactly. They were certain that God was pleased when He looked at them, all decked out in the fine deeds they had done.

For example, the Pharisees knew that God's Law said, "Do not murder." They would never kill another person. They believed they had kept God's Law in all its details. But

Jesus knew that they often hated their brothers and spoke to them in anger. Jesus said their goodness was full of holes. *Put on the shirt.*

The Pharisees couldn't please God with their own goodness. They sinned every day. When we look at ourselves, we see that we sin every day too. No matter how hard we try, our goodness—our righteousness—like theirs, is full of dirt and holes. It will never be good enough for God.

Jesus took away the dirty clothes of our sins when He died for us on the cross. *Take off the shirt and stuff it back in the bag.* He dressed us, instead, in His own righteousness. Now when God looks at us, He sees the perfect righteousness of His Son, Jesus.

Dressed in Jesus' righteousness, God's Holy Spirit helps us love our brothers and sisters as Jesus loves us, show respect for our own bodies and those of others, and speak truthfully and keep our word to one another.

Prayer: Dear Heavenly Father, no matter how hard we try to obey You, we sin. Our own righteousness will never be enough to please You. Forgive our sins for Jesus' sake. Dress us in His perfect righteousness and help us live lives that are pleasing to You. In Jesus' name we pray. Amen.

Friends and Enemies

SEVENTH SUNDAY AFTER THE EPIPHANY: Matt. 5:38–48

Text: But I tell you: Love your enemies and pray for those who persecute you, that you may be sons of your Father in heaven. *Matt. 5:44–45a*

Teaching aids: Three boy puppets. These can be as simple as cutting pictures of three boys from a magazine and pasting them on craft sticks. If you wish, more elaborate puppets may be made or ready-made puppets may be used.

Gospel truth: God loves us so much, He will help us love others, even our enemies.

Today I want to tell you a story about two friends. This is Barney. *Ask one child to hold up the first puppet.* And this is Clifford. *Ask another child to hold up the second puppet.* Barney and Clifford live in the same apartment building and do everything together. They ride their bikes together. They walk to school together. They play soccer and baseball together. They are the best of friends.

One day another boy moves into the same apartment building. His name is Theo. *Ask a third child to hold up the third puppet.* Barney and Clifford think Theo might like to ride bikes with them, so they knock on his door. Theo is glad to meet some new friends, and the three boys ride off together.

After a few days, Barney and Theo start riding their bikes and walking to school and playing soccer by themselves. *Have the children holding the Barney and Theo pup-*

pets stand together. They forgot all about Clifford. *Have the child holding the Clifford puppet stand alone.* How do you think Clifford feels about that? *Allow time for the children to answer, then collect the puppets.*

As time goes by, things get worse for Clifford. One day when he is walking to school alone, he sees Barney and Theo up ahead of him. "Wait for me," he calls and starts running toward the two boys. Barney and Theo laugh and run away from Clifford—faster and faster. Clifford stops running. He feels so sad.

Another day Barney and Theo throw rocks at Clifford. Another day they push him down. And one time they even steal his bike. Instead of being his friends, Barney and Theo become Clifford's enemies. What do you think Clifford will do next? *Allow time for the children's suggestions.*

In the Bible, Jesus tells us, "Love your enemies." That's hard to do, isn't it? It's hard to love people who hurt us and make fun of us and are mean to us. But that's what Jesus does for us. He just keeps on loving us no matter how many times we hurt Him when we tell a lie or talk back to our parents or are mean to a brother or sister. He loves us so much that He even died to suffer the punishment for all our sins. Even on the cross He did not get mad at the enemies who put Him there. That's a whole lot of love. Remembering Jesus' love for us can help us love and forgive the people who hurt us.

Jesus also tells us to pray for those people who hurt us and make fun of us and are mean to us. Ask Jesus to help you love them. Ask Jesus to help you be kind to them even when they are mean to you. Jesus will hear your prayer, and He will help you.

Prayer: Dear Jesus, help us love everyone, even those people who hurt us and make fun of us and are mean to us. Please listen, Jesus, as each of us comes to You in silent prayer for someone we need Your help to love. Dear Jesus, please help me love … *Allow a short time for silent prayer.* Help me love this person just like You love me. In Your name we pray. Amen.

Me? Worry?

EIGHTH SUNDAY AFTER THE EPIPHANY:
Matt. 6:24–34

Text: But seek first His kingdom and His righteousness, and all these things will be given to you as well. *Matt. 6:33*

Teaching aids: Cut out a completely white paper flower, including a white stem. If there are not flowers on the altar, bring a bouquet of real flowers. Also have available a picture or figurine of a bird.

Gospel truth: God, who takes such good care of the birds and flowers, takes even better care of us, His own children. So instead of worrying about earthly matters, God helps us keep our minds focused on Him and His kingdom.

I brought a flower with me today. *Hold up the white paper flower.* Does this look like a real flower? What's wrong with it? You're right. My flower doesn't have any color at all. It's all white. Real flowers have lots of colors, and they always have green stems.

Point out the bouquet of flowers on the altar or hold up your bouquet. What colors do you see in these flowers? *Let the children name colors.* These flowers don't make their own colors. God does. God makes all the flowers and dresses each one of them in bright colors. One time Jesus said that even the richest king in the whole world never had clothes as beautiful as the flowers. God gives them just what they need.

Hold up the bird. This bird flies high in the sky. Does she work hard to plant her food? Does she gather her food into barns? No, when she's hungry, she finds some seeds or a juicy worm to eat. God gives her all the food she needs.

Do you think the flowers worry about their colors? Do the birds worry about their worms? No, they don't. But sometimes we worry about our lives. We worry that our clothing isn't nice enough. Or we worry that our friend won't invite us to a party. Or we worry about those math problems that are so hard to figure out.

We don't need to worry about our clothes or our food or our schoolwork. We don't need to worry about anything at all! God loves His creation very much. He dresses the flowers in beautiful colors. He gives the birds food to eat. If God takes such good care of the birds and the flowers, we know He will take good care of us. God loves us more than anything! We are His own children. He even sent Jesus to die and rise to win us life with Him in heaven.

God gives us His Holy Spirit to remind us how much He loves us. God knows we need clothes and food and friends. We can trust Him. He'll see that we have everything we need so we can focus our thoughts and actions on Him.

Prayer: Dear God, You dress the flowers in beautiful colors, and You feed the birds when they are hungry. Help us trust in You. Keep us thinking about You and Your love instead of worrying about our own needs and problems. Thank You for loving us so much. In Jesus' name we pray. Amen.

Special Friends

THE TRANSFIGURATION OF OUR LORD: Matt. 17:1–9

Text: After six days Jesus took with Him Peter, James and John the brother of James, and led them up a high mountain by themselves. *Matt. 17:1*

Teaching aid: A large mirror.

Gospel truth: Jesus, our Savior, is our best friend. He will be with us always and will help us when we are sad or have problems.

Friends are important to all of us. Friends get a big smile on their face when they see us. Friends laugh with us when we tell a funny—or not so funny—joke. Friends are there to help us when we feel sad or have problems. Friends like to do things with us. What do you like to do with your friends? *Allow time for the children to respond.*

Jesus had many friends when He lived on earth preaching and teaching. But three of His disciples—Peter, James, and John—often were chosen to be with Jesus at special times. I guess you could call them Jesus' special friends. They were there when Jesus healed a little girl, and they were there when Jesus felt so sad as He prayed in the Garden of Gethsemane.

One time Peter, James, and John went with Jesus to the top of a high mountain. Peter, James, and John couldn't believe their eyes! Jesus' face shone like the sun, and His clothes became as white as light. Jesus showed Peter, James, and John how He looked in heaven. Then all at once Moses and Elijah appeared with Jesus on the mountain and started talking to Him. Peter wanted this special time with Jesus to last longer, so He offered to make three shelters for Jesus and Moses and Elijah to stay in.

Just then a voice spoke from a cloud. "This is My Son, whom I love; with Him I am well pleased." It was God the Father talking to them! Then the voice said one more thing to Peter, James, and John. "Listen to Him!" God said.

Listen to Him! God told these three friends of Jesus to listen to Him. Listening to Jesus must be very important if God Himself told Peter, James, and John to do it. How can we listen to Jesus? *Allow the children to suggest ways they can listen to Jesus, such as reading the Bible, going to church, attending Sunday school, and listening to Bible stories.*

When we listen to Jesus, we learn how much He loves us. We find out that Jesus is our special friend too. *Hold up the mirror so the children's faces are reflected in it.* This mirror shows some of Jesus' special friends. Do you see them? Jesus loves all these boys and girls so much. He wants to be with each one of them all the time. He wants to help them when they are sad or have problems. Jesus is their best friend. *Continue to hold up the mirror as you read the poem below.*

> I have a friend who loves me so;
> He's by my side each place I go.
> He always knows just how I feel.
> He's always there at every meal.
> If I'm chasing the wind or riding my bike,
> Or skating so fast or trying to hike,
> My friend is there. He wouldn't hide.
> Open His arms; I'm safe inside.
> Can you guess who loves without end?
> You've heard His name—Jesus, my friend.

Prayer: Dear Jesus, thank You for all my friends—old friends and new friends, big friends and little friends, tall friends and short friends. And thank You, Jesus, for always being my best friend of all. In Your name we pray. Amen.

Breads
and Bibles

⟹◇⟸

FIRST SUNDAY IN LENT: Matt. 4:1–11

Text: Jesus answered, "It is written: 'Man does not live on bread alone, but on every word that comes from the mouth of God.' " *Matt. 4:4*

Teaching aids: A loaf of bread and a Bible. *Optional:* A tortilla and/or pita bread, bagel and/or doughnut.

Gospel truth: God gives us food both for bodily needs and spiritual ones. God's gift of His Word strengthens us, guides us, and gives us the promise of eternal life.

The other day when I was walking down the street, I felt really hungry because it was late in the afternoon and I still hadn't had any lunch. My stomach was growling and making all sorts of strange noises. All I could think about was getting something to eat. Have you ever felt like that?

I smelled all sorts of wonderful scents coming from a store just a few doors down the street. I started walking faster and faster and faster until I stood right in front of a window filled with all kinds of delicious baked goods. I saw apple pie and oatmeal-raisin cookies and chocolate layer cake sitting next to gooey cinnamon rolls and chocolate éclairs. I hurried up to the counter and bought my favorite thing to eat from the bakery. What do you think I bought? *Allow time for the children to respond, than hold up a loaf of bread.* I bought a loaf of bread. I just love fresh-baked bread. It's one of my favorite foods.

People all over the world eat bread. Some breads are

square. *Hold up a slice of bread.* Some breads are flat. *Show a tortilla and/or pita bread.* Some breads have a hole in the middle. *Show a bagel and/or a doughnut.* But all breads taste good and nourish your body. Bread helps your body grow and stay strong.

But Jesus said that people can't live on bread alone. He told us about another "food" that is even more important in our lives. What do you think that "food" could be?

That "food" is God's Word. *Hold up the Bible.* When we listen to God's Word and hear what God is saying to us, His Word nourishes us and helps us grow in a different way than this bread does. God's Word tells us how Jesus came to earth to be our Savior. As we follow Jesus' loving example, we grow stronger so we are able to say no when we are tempted to do something wrong. God's Word helps us grow wiser so we are able to make wise decisions in our lives. And it helps us grow in love for each other. Most importantly, God's Word shows us the way to live forever with Him in heaven.

This bread *(hold up the loaf)* helps our bodies grow bigger and taller. But this Bible *(hold up the Bible)* gives us a gift much better than that. The Bible tells us God loves us so much that He sent Jesus to save us from our sins. And because we believe in Jesus, we too will live forever in heaven. That's the best gift of all!

Prayer: Dear God, thank You for the nourishing bread you give us to eat. Even more, thank You for giving us Your Word to help us grow stronger and wiser and more loving. Most of all, thank You for sending Jesus to save us from our sins and give us the gift of life forever in heaven. In His name we pray. Amen.

What Would Jesus Do?

⇒•⇐

SECOND SUNDAY IN LENT: John 4:5–26

Text: The Samaritan woman said to Him, "You are a Jew and I am a Samaritan woman. How can you ask me for a drink?" (For Jews do not associate with Samaritans.) *John 4:9*

Teaching aids: A clear glass filled with water and an earthenware jug or clay flowerpot.

Gospel truth: Jesus, who loves everyone, will help us love others too.

Hold up the glass of water. When you are so-o-o thirsty for a cool glass of water, what do you do? *Allow the children to respond.* That's right. It's easy for us to get water whenever we want some. We just turn on the faucet and the water comes streaming out.

Long ago when the Bible was written, people had to work much harder to get a glass of water. Every evening when it was cooler, the women of the village had to walk to the well for water. The well, dug deep into the ground, was an important part of village life. The women carried big earthenware jugs made of clay. *Show the earthenware jug or flowerpot.* After they filled their jugs with water, they would balance the heavy pots on top of their heads or shoulders and carry them home. It was hard—but important—work.

One day Jesus stopped to rest by a well. He was so-o-o thirsty. When a woman came to the well to get some water,

Jesus asked her, "Will you give me a drink?" The woman looked at Jesus in surprise. She couldn't believe He was talking to her. After all, she was a woman, and in those days, religious teachers hardly ever spoke to a woman in public. And, to make it even more surprising, she was a Samaritan. The Jewish people did not like the Samaritan people at all and tried to avoid them whenever they could.

But Jesus didn't care that He was speaking in public to a woman, and He didn't care that she was a Samaritan. Jesus loved her and wanted to tell her about the way to heaven. So He did. And do you know what happened? The woman believed in Jesus. And she told many others about Him, and they believed too.

We meet Samaritan women in our lives too. Oh, they aren't from a country called Samaria and they might not be women, but they are people we don't want to be friends with. Maybe it's a big kid who lives down the street who always teases you. Or maybe it's someone at school who tries to pick fights with you at recess. Or maybe it's someone you'd just rather not sit next to at lunch or on the school bus.

Next time you find yourself wanting to avoid someone who's a little bit different than you, remember Jesus and the Samaritan woman. Then stop and pray, "Jesus, what would you do?" What do you think Jesus might do? *Allow the children to offer ideas of what Jesus would do. Look for answers stressing love and acceptance.*

Jesus loves everyone. He doesn't care if we are Jewish or Samaritan. He doesn't care if we are black or white or pink or purple. He doesn't care if we are young or old or tall or short. Jesus loves us just the way we are. He loves us so much He gave His life for us. Jesus will help us love other people too.

Prayer: Dear Jesus, sometimes we find it hard to love other people the way you do. Help us, Jesus, to remember how much You love everyone. Help us love others too. In Your name we pray. Amen.

Whenever and Wherever

———⫸◆⫷———

THIRD SUNDAY IN LENT: John 9:13–17, 34–39

Text: Now the day on which Jesus had made the mud and opened the man's eyes was a Sabbath. ... Some of the Pharisees said, "This man is not from God, for He does not keep the Sabbath." *John 9:14, 16*

Teaching aids: A doll with an adhesive bandage on its knee.

Gospel truth: Jesus healed and helped people whenever and wherever He found them. He is always ready to help us too.

Hold up the doll. This is Clarabelle. Clarabelle doesn't feel well today. When she woke up this morning her nose felt all stuffy. Then after breakfast her stomach hurt. And when she was getting ready for church, Clarabelle fell down and scraped her knee. She started crying.

Poor Clarabelle. *Place the doll over your shoulder and pat her on the back.* She felt so sad. She thought no one cared about her. Then her father heard her crying and gave her a big hug. He washed Clarabelle's knee and put this bandage on it. *Show the bandage on the doll's knee.* I think she feels a little better now.

Did you ever have a morning like Clarabelle's? *Let the children tell their stories.* I suppose now and then we all have a bad morning like that. Hopefully, it's not a Sunday morning.

The Bible tells us about a Sabbath morning long ago

when Jesus helped a blind man. On that morning, Jesus put some mud on the blind man's eyes. Then Jesus told the man to go and wash off the mud. When the blind man washed the mud off of his eyes, he could see! For the first time in his whole life the man could see the blue sky and yellow flowers and green grass. He could see the faces of his family. He could even see Jesus smiling at him. What a miracle that was!

But there was a problem. Some of the church leaders called Pharisees were upset because Jesus helped the blind man to see on the Sabbath day. The word that *Sabbath* comes from in the Hebrew language means "to stop" or "quit." The Sabbath day was a day of complete rest. No work at all was to be done. The people were not allowed to gather food or chop wood or even cook.

The Pharisees tried to make sure that everyone followed this law—and other laws—exactly. They didn't like it at all when Jesus healed the blind man on the Sabbath day. They were angry at Jesus. And they were angry at the blind man for believing in Him.

But Jesus didn't care what the Pharisees said about Him. He knew that the blind man needed His help, and He helped him. Jesus didn't stop caring about people just because it was the Sabbath day. If someone needed His help, He helped that person.

Jesus helped people wherever and whenever He found them. One time He told a man who couldn't walk to "Get up, pick up your bed, and go home." Right away, the man could walk and run and even jump.

Another time a worried father ran up to Jesus. "Please help my little boy," the father said. "He is so sick."

"Go home," Jesus said. "Your little boy is well." And he was! The boy had gotten well at the same time Jesus had told the father that his son was better.

Jesus helped many, many more people who were sick or sad or hurting. Jesus always cared about them, no matter what day of the week it was. And Jesus cares about you too.

He cares about you on Monday and Tuesday and Wednesday and Thursday and Friday and Saturday and Sunday. Jesus *always* cares. He's *always* there to help. Let's thank Him for His love.

Prayer: Thank You, Jesus, for always caring for us. No matter what day of the week it is, You are always there to help us. Thank You, dear Jesus. Thank You for Your love. In Your name we pray. Amen.

That's Great!

FOURTH SUNDAY IN LENT: Matt. 20:17–28

Text: Whoever wants to become great among you must be your servant, and whoever wants to be first must be your slave—just as the Son of Man did not come to be served, but to serve, and to give His life for a ransom for many. *Matt. 20:26–28*

Teaching aids: A paper crown (a fast-food restaurant will probably give you one), several dollar bills, a football and/or basketball, and a jar of bubbles.

Gospel truth: Jesus gave His life for us. His life is the supreme example of a life lived in service to others. True greatness can only be found when Jesus' love shines through us in service to others.

Did you ever wish you were a great person? Have you ever dreamed you were famous and did wonderful things in the world? *Place the paper crown on your head.* Maybe you wanted to be a king or a queen. Then everyone in your kingdom would bow down whenever you walked by, and everyone would have to do just what you told them to.

Hold up the dollar bills. Maybe you wished you were the richest person in the world. You had lots and lots of dollars—so many dollars that you could buy anything you wanted. Then you could just walk in the toy store and buy armfuls and armfuls of toys. You could even buy the whole toy store!

Hold up the football and/or basketball. Or maybe you dreamed you were a sports star. In every game you played, you scored the most points. The crowds cheered and cheered. When you weren't playing football or basketball, you wore your favorite tennis shoes and made a television commercial!

Some people might say that kings and rich people and sports stars are great people. And maybe they are. But Jesus says something else about how to become a great person. Let me read you a verse from the Bible. Jesus says, "Whoever wants to become great among you must be your servant."

What does Jesus say is the way to be great? *Allow the children to answer. If necessary, read Jesus' words again. Help them understand that Jesus is telling us that being a servant is the way to be great.* When Jesus says that to be great we need to become servants, He doesn't mean that we should let others order us around. Being a servant means showing love to others and helping them with whatever they need.

What Jesus says about greatness may be different from our dreams of greatness. But Jesus knows what He's talking about. Jesus is the greatest person who ever lived. He's the King of kings, Lord of lords, Light of the world, and the Son of God. And Jesus, the greatest person who ever lived, Himself became a servant when He gave His life for us on the cross.

When we let Jesus' love fill our hearts, His love bubbles right out of us into the world. *Blow some bubbles with the bubble mixture.* Then we can show His love to everyone we see. We can serve other people the way Jesus asks us to. Jesus makes us great!

Try to do at least one "serving" act today. Remember how much Jesus loves you and let His love come bubbling right out. Can you name a way you could show love to someone today? *Allow the children to answer. Suggestions might include reading a story to a younger brother or sister, helping a friend, or setting the table for dinner.* Those are all *great* ideas from lots of *great* servants.

Prayer: Dear Jesus, sometimes it's hard to understand what You tell us about greatness when the world tells us something different. Thank You, dear Jesus, for showing us what true greatness really is. Let Your love fill our hearts and bubble over in service to others. In Your name we pray. Amen.

What's Faith?

➤◆⬅

FIFTH SUNDAY IN LENT: John 11:1–53

Text: Jesus said to her, "I am the resurrection and the life. He who believes in Me will live, even though he dies; and whoever lives and believes in me will never die. Do you believe this?" "Yes, Lord," she told Him, "I believe that You are the Christ, the Son of God, who was to come into the world." *John 11:25–27*

Teaching aid: An empty mug.

Gospel truth: God is alive and with us even though we can't see, hear (in the conventional sense), taste, touch, or smell Him.

Hold up the mug but don't let the children see inside it. This mug is filled with something I like a lot. It's something I can't live without. And it's something I always have around me. Can you guess what it is? *Allow the children to guess what's in the mug.* Those are all good guesses. Now would you like to see what's inside my mug? *Lower the mug and let the children peek inside.* What do you see? *Allow them to answer "nothing."*

That's right, you don't see anything inside my mug. But there's something there all right. It fills every inch of my mug. My mug is filled with … air.

We can't see air at all. We can't smell or taste air. But we know it's there. It's just as real as water or land. Air covers the whole world. Without air, there would be no life on earth. Every living plant and animal needs air to survive. You can live for a long time without food and a few days without water, but no person can live more than a few minutes without air.

We can't see God either. We also can't smell, taste, touch, or hear Him in the normal way. But we know God is there. God's Holy Spirit helps us believe in Him even though we can't see Him. That's called faith. God put faith in our hearts when we were baptized.

Even though we can't see air, we can see what it does. We see the air moving sailboats across the water. We feel the air pushing against us when it blows in the wind. We know it's real.

We also see, touch, hear, smell, and taste the things God does. We watch leaves grow on trees and feel the warm sun on our backs. We hear birds singing and rain falling on the roof. We smell the roses blooming and taste all the good foods He gives to us. But only in His Word can we learn all about God.

In the Bible, God tells us who He is and what He has done for us. As we learn God's Word, His Holy Spirit helps our faith grow strong. The Bible tells us about a time Jesus asked a woman named Martha if she believed in Him. Martha loved Jesus. So Martha said, "Yes, Lord. I believe that you are the Christ, the Son of God, who was to come into the world." That's faith!

Let's say Martha's words of faith together. *Say Martha's words as indicated below. Each time you stop, let the children repeat the words.* Yes, Lord. *Stop.* I believe. *Stop.* That You are the Christ. *Stop.* The Son of God. *Stop.* Who was to come into the world. *Stop.* As you listen to the sermon today, see if you can hear the words *believe* and *faith.* Let's thank God for giving us a strong faith in Him.

Prayer: Dear God, we want to thank You for making Yourself known to us. Help us study the Bible so that we may learn more and more about You and Your love for us. In Jesus' name we pray. Amen.

Bad News and Good News

====>◆<====

PALM SUNDAY: Matt. 27:11–54

Text: Then they led Him away to crucify Him. *Matt. 27:31*

"Surely He was the Son of God!" *Matt. 27:54*

Teaching aids: A newspaper, a piece of red cloth, large nails, a crucifix, an empty cross, and a crown of thorns. (To make a crown of thorns, wind two rose or citrus branches around each other. Or cut one out of brown construction paper and paste or draw "thorns" on it.) If possible have a small cross for each child to take home.

Gospel truth: Jesus died to take the punishment for our sins and rose again on the third day. God's Holy Spirit gives us sure faith in Christ and the assurance of eternal life.

This morning on my way to church, I stopped and bought a newspaper. *Hold up the newspaper.* Newspapers are full of news. Do you know what the word *news* means? *Allow the children to give their best definition.* News is information about something that has happened.

Unfortunately, often the news we hear is bad news. We hear stories about hurricanes or wars or people hurting other people. That news makes us sad. But there's another kind of news—news that makes us happy. It's called *good* news. Those are the stories about people helping people or good weather forecasts or babies being born.

The week between Palm Sunday and Easter Sunday is

filled with both bad news and good news. We feel sad because of all the bad things that happened to Jesus. It makes us sad that people put a red robe around His shoulders (*hold up the red cloth*) and placed a crown of thorns on His head. *Hold up the crown of thorns.* It makes us sad that people spat on Jesus and hit Him and made fun of Him. It especially makes us sad that people nailed Jesus (*hold up the nails*) to a wooden cross. *Hold up the crucifix.* Jesus stayed on that cross until He died.

We might think all those sad things are bad news. But actually they happened on a day called "Good" Friday. Good Friday is a day filled with both bad news and good news. The bad news is that Jesus suffered and died. But the good news is that He did it all to save us from our sins. Now we have forgiveness. We still feel sad because Jesus had to suffer and die, but we are happy because it means we are saved from all our sins.

But Good Friday isn't the only day filled with news this week. *Hold up the empty cross next to the crucifix.* What's different about this cross? *Allow the children to answer.* That's right, this cross is empty. It's empty because Jesus didn't stay on the cross. Three days after He died, He came alive again. The empty cross reminds us of the happiest, best news day of all—Easter Sunday. That's the day Jesus rose from the dead. We know Jesus will always be with us. He'll always love us. And someday we'll live forever with Him in heaven. That's a good news day!

Give each child a cross to take home. I'm going to give each of you this empty cross to remind you of Jesus this week. Whenever you see this cross, God's Holy Spirit will help you remember Jesus. Remember He died on Good Friday to save you from all your sins. Remember He came alive again on Easter. Remember how much He loves you.

Then read the following verses from the song "Do You Know Who Died for Me?" as a closing activity. Ask the children to call out "Jesus" after you ask them a question.

Do you know who died for me? "Jesus."
Lovingly He died for me, yes, He really did!
Do you know who rose for me? "Jesus."
Lovingly He rose for me, yes, He really did!

Prayer: Lead a short prayer thanking Jesus for His saving work.

The Happiest Day of the Year

———◆———

THE RESURRECTION OF OUR LORD:
Matt. 28:1–10

Text: The angel said to the women, "Do not be afraid, for I know that you are looking for Jesus, who was crucified. He is not here; He has risen, just as He said." *Matt. 28:5–6*

Teaching aids: Long strips of paper with one of the following sentences written on each strip: "He is risen." "Jesus is alive." "He is risen indeed." "Alleluia!" "Jesus lives." "Christ the Lord is risen today." "I know that my Redeemer lives." Acquire enough empty plastic eggs that you can give one to each child. Place the paper strips and the plastic eggs inside a box and gift-wrap the box.

Gospel truth: Jesus rose from the dead on Easter Sunday, the happiest day of the year.

When I came to church this morning, this present was sitting on my desk. *Place the gift-wrapped box on your lap.* I think someone might be a little confused. After all, this is Easter morning not Christmas morning. Oh well, I like presents any time of the year.

What do you think is inside this box? *Allow the children to guess.* Those all sound like good presents. Shall I unwrap the box and see what's inside? *Unwrap the gift and open the box. Show the children the eggs and paper strips inside.* The whole box is filled with plastic eggs, and here on top are some paper streamers. The paper streamers have some words on them. Let's see what they say. *Remove the paper strips from the box. Ask volunteers to read them aloud one at a time.* Those are wonderful messages, aren't they?

Now I know why this present was left on my desk. Easter is the day when Jesus rose from the dead. That means He came alive again after He had died on the cross to pay the price for our sins. Because Jesus lives, we will live forever in heaven. And that's the best present of all! I think Easter is the happiest day of the whole year.

Look at all the eggs in this box! I'm going to give one to each of you. *Give each child one plastic egg.* Go ahead and open your eggs. What's inside? *Allow the children to answer.* That's right—there's nothing inside the eggs. That's because when Mary Magdalene and the other Mary went to Jesus' tomb on that first Easter, Jesus wasn't there. The tomb was empty. Jesus was alive!

An angel sitting next to the tomb told the women, "Do not be afraid, for I know that you are looking for Jesus, who was crucified. He is not here; He has risen, just as He said." What a wonderful, happy surprise those words were for the two women. When they looked inside Jesus' tomb, it was empty. When you look inside your egg, it's empty. The empty egg reminds us of the empty tomb that first Easter Sunday.

Other things remind us of that first Easter too—butterflies bursting out of brown cocoons. Red, yellow, and blue flowers popping out of the ground from dried-up bulbs. New green leaves growing out of tiny buds. These things remind us of that first Easter when Jesus rose from the dead to give us new life. What a happy, happy day that was.

Whenever you look inside your empty egg, remember that Jesus is alive! And whenever you see a butterfly or daffodil or new green leaves, remember Jesus is alive! During the sermon and the rest of the service listen for the word *Alleluia. Alleluia* is a happy word that means "praise God." Whenever you hear the word *Alleluia* in church today, remember Jesus is alive!

Conclude by reading the following poem.
　　　It's the happiest day of the year.
　　　Christ the Lord is risen today.
　　　Listen carefully. Do you hear?
　　　"Alleluia!" the people say.
　　　"Alleluia! Alleluia! Alleluia!"

Prayer: Lead a prayer praising God for giving us His Son as our Savior.

Real Peace

SECOND SUNDAY OF EASTER:
John 20:19–31

Text: Jesus came and stood among them and said, "Peace be with you!" *John 20:19*

Teaching aids: The word *peace* written on a large piece of poster board; a picture of a busy city with lots of traffic and people; a picture of a calm nature scene (an ocean, mountains, or fields). Draw a "calm" picture with a simple, wavy design in soft blues and greens. Draw a "busy" picture with lots of intersecting lines and sharp angles in bright, strong colors. Have a marker available.

Gospel truth: Because of Jesus' death and resurrection, we enjoy true peace. We know that Jesus has won the victory over death, and we will live forever with Him in heaven.

We often hear the phrase "Peace be with you" here in church. What do those words mean to you? *Allow the children to answer. This will be a difficult concept for children. Acknowledge all answers.*

Hold up the poster. Peace is a hard word to explain, isn't it? It's not like *dog* or *cat* or even *run* or *jump*. We can take someone to see a real dog or a cat, and we can show them how we run or jump, but we can't do that with *peace*. We can't see or touch peace. We can't taste it or smell it. It's just something we feel inside.

Hold up the picture of the busy city. Do you think this picture shows peace? *Allow the children to respond. Hold up the picture of the calm nature scene.* Do you think this picture shows peace? *Allow the children to respond and give reasons.*

Hold up the calm drawing. Does this picture look peaceful to you? *After the children answer, hold up the busy drawing.* Does this picture look peaceful to you? *Allow the children to respond.*

We usually think of peace as being something calm and quiet, don't we, sort of like these two pictures. *Hold up the nature picture and the calm drawing.* Peace makes us feel gentle and happy. It makes us feel relaxed and confident. It gives us a feeling that everything is under control.

On the evening of the first Easter, the disciples sat together in a locked room. They didn't feel peaceful at all. They were afraid the same people who had killed Jesus might come and hurt them. All of a sudden Jesus stood in the room with them. He was alive! And do you know the first thing Jesus said to them? *Hold up the poster.* He said "Peace be with you!"

Jesus didn't want His disciples to be afraid. He wanted them to feel peace. Jesus wanted to give His disciples a special kind of peace that only He can give. This special peace came from knowing that Jesus died and was alive again. Because Jesus was alive, the disciples didn't have to be afraid and could be sure that they would go to heaven and be with Him forever.

We too can feel the peace that only Jesus gives. *Hold up the poster.* His peace is a wonderful gift. It fills our lives with happiness. We can feel Jesus' peace because we know that He died to save us from our sins. *Draw a cross next to the word* peace. He came alive again on the third day. *Draw a butterfly outline next to the word* peace.

Listen for the word *peace* throughout the sermon and the church service. When you hear it, remember that no matter what happens in our lives, no matter how confused or sad or without peace we might feel, we can feel happy and calm because we know that Jesus is alive. He is with us to help us when we are afraid. He promises us that we will live forever with Him in heaven. That's real peace! The kind that only Jesus can give.

Prayer: Dear Jesus, thank You for being our Savior. Please give us Your special peace. Fill our hearts with quiet and calm because we know that no matter what happens, we are Your children. We are saved. In Your name we pray. Amen.

Wonderful Words from God

THIRD SUNDAY OF EASTER: Luke 24:13–35

Text: And beginning with Moses and all the Prophets, He explained to them what was said in all the Scriptures concerning Himself. ... They asked each other, "Were not our hearts burning within us while He talked with us on the road and opened the Scriptures to us?" *Luke 24:27, 32*

Teaching aids: Several pieces of mail, a Bible, a pretend letter from God (copy this letter and put it in an envelope addressed to "The Boys and Girls of [*your church name*]").

Dear Boys and Girls,

    I am writing this letter to tell you that I love you. You are all My special children. I love you so much that I sent Jesus to die for your sins. But Jesus didn't stay dead. I raised Him up again on the first Easter Sunday. Because of Jesus, you have new life, and someday you will live forever with Me in heaven.

Love,

God

Gospel truth: God gave us His Word to show us the way to eternal life through the saving work of His Son.

    Hold up several pieces of mail, including the pretend letter from God. Look at all the letters the mail carrier delivered to church yesterday. *Briefly go through the mail. For example, say, "Here's a bill from the telephone company. And here's a letter from a missionary in South America." Stop when you come to the letter from God.* What's this? This letter looks interesting. Look, it's addressed to "The Boys and Girls of *(your church name)*." Shall I open it and see what it says? *Open the letter.* I'll read it to you. *Read the letter aloud.*

This letter gives us some very good news. It makes us feel happy, doesn't it? This is just a make-believe letter, but we know that everything this letter says is true. We know it's true because God has already written us a *real* letter. *Hold up the Bible.* It's called the Bible.

The Bible is God's real, true letter to us. In it, He tells us everything He wants us to know. He tells us how much He loves us. He tells us about our best friend, Jesus. He tells us how we can live with Him forever in heaven. The Bible is our wonderful letter from God.

Long ago many different men wrote the Bible, but God gave them the thoughts and words. The Bible is God's Word. *Show the Old Testament.* This part of God's Word is called the Old Testament. It was written before the birth of Jesus. *Show the New Testament.* This part is called the New Testament. It was written after the birth of Jesus. The more we study His Word, the more God's Holy Spirit teaches us about God's love for us in Jesus.

After Jesus rose from the dead, He appeared to two men walking down the road to a village called Emmaus. The men didn't recognize Jesus. But as they walked, Jesus talked to the men about the Bible. He told them about some of God's Old Testament helpers—Moses, Isaiah, Jeremiah, Ezekiel, and Daniel. Jesus told them what God's Word had to say about Him. The two men loved listening to Jesus. When they reached the village, they asked Jesus to stay with them for dinner. At dinner when Jesus gave them some bread, the men realized who He was.

Then Jesus disappeared. When the two men looked at each other, they said, "Were not our hearts burning within us while He talked with us on the road and opened the Scriptures to us?" When Jesus told them about the Bible it made the two men feel so happy and excited they felt like their hearts were on fire. That's what God's Word does. It fills our hearts with joy and brings us closer to Jesus.

Act out the following poem with the children.

The Bible is God's special book,
> *(Cup your hands to form an open book.)*

And He has told us where to look,
> *(Point to an open "page" on one hand.)*

To find out all we need to know
> *(Make sweeping circles with your arms.)*

About the love He has to show.
> *(Cross your arms on your chest.)*

When I listen and really hear,
> *(Point to your ears.)*

I know that God is always near.
> *(Bring both palms toward your shoulders.)*

And when I look and really see,
> *(Point to your eyes.)*

I know God loves you and me.
> *(Point to others and then to yourself.)*

From *Close to Jesus*, by Elizabeth Friedrich. © 1992 Concordia Publishing House.

Prayer: Thank You, dear God, for giving us Your wonderful Words. Send Your Holy Spirit to help us study, love, and follow Your Word all our lives. In Jesus' name we pray. Amen.

The Good Shepherd

FOURTH SUNDAY OF EASTER: John 10:1–10

Text: He calls his own sheep by name and leads them out. When he has brought out all his own, he goes on ahead of them, and his sheep follow him because they know his voice. *John 10:3–4*

Teaching aids: A cloak or blanket; a rod—use a short, thick, club-like piece of wood; a staff—use a straight, long stick; a flute, recorder, or other woodwind instrument; a cloth bag filled with a few stones, some raisins, and some bread.

Gospel truth: Jesus is our Good Shepherd. He cares for us and loves us so much that He gave His life for us. He leads us to life in heaven with Him.

Put the cloak or blanket around your shoulders and carry the rod, staff, flute, and bag. Can any of you guess what I am dressed to look like? *Allow the children to guess.* I'm a shepherd. Many people worked as shepherds in Bible times. What does a shepherd do? *Allow the children to answer.* Sheep were very important animals in Bible times. They could survive in the wilderness and could climb the steep hills.

Sheep are easily scared, and they don't trust people very much. When they are scared, they run away because they can't defend themselves. But they do trust their shepherd. They know the sound of his voice, and they follow him. So every morning, the shepherd would go to the sheep pen and call his sheep. Then he would walk in front of the sheep and lead them to find food and water.

The shepherd would search for the best pasture for his sheep. Sometimes he had to lead the sheep down narrow paths in the mountains to find that grassy spot. Then the shepherd would lead his sheep to quiet streams where they could drink the clean, clear water.

While the sheep ate grass, the shepherd might play some music on his flute. *Hold up the instrument.* When he got hungry, he might enjoy some lunch from his bag. *Take some raisins and bread out of the bag.*

If one of the sheep started to wander away from the flock, the shepherd would use his staff (*show the children the staff*) to guide that sheep back to the others. Sometimes wild animals would threaten his sheep. Then the shepherd used his rod (*show the rod*) or some stones (*show the stones from the bag*) to scare away the wolves or bears.

At night, the shepherd led his sheep back home. He walked ahead of his sheep and gently called them by name. The sheep followed him back to the sheep pen because they knew his voice. The pen was surrounded by brush or stone walls and had only one gate. This way the shepherd could guard the gate and protect the sheep from wild animals or thieves or robbers. As the sheep walked into the pen, the shepherd counted them to make sure each sheep was safe. If even one sheep was missing, the shepherd would climb back up the mountain and search until he found the missing sheep.

Jesus is our Good Shepherd. He loves us and takes care of us just as the shepherd in Bible times loved and cared for his sheep. Jesus knows your name too. He says, "(*Call several children by name*), you are Mine. I love you." Jesus knows all of your names and loves you and cares for you.

We listen to Jesus' voice, just as the sheep listened to the voice of their shepherd. We hear Jesus' voice in the Bible. He tells us that He loves us and cares for us. Jesus' voice tells us that He died on the cross to win us forgiveness and eternal life. He leads us to heaven. That's really being a Good Shepherd!

Prayer: Dear Jesus, thank You for being our Good Shepherd. Thank You for caring for us and watching over us. Thank You for loving us so much that You gave Your life for us. Help us listen to Your voice. Help us follow You. In Your name we pray. Amen

Marking the Way

───◦◈◦───

FIFTH SUNDAY OF EASTER: John 14:1–12

Text: Jesus answered, "I am the way and the truth and the life. No one comes to the Father except through Me." *John 14:6*

Teaching aids: Three clues written and hidden around the church for a treasure hunt. Clues might read, "I am the special place where people get baptized." A clue at the baptismal font could read, "I am the person who makes music." The organist could have a clue reading, "I am the place where people come into the church." The treasure (a basket or treasure chest of treats—stickers, bookmarks, wrapped candy, etc.) can be placed at the church door or wherever else your clues lead the children.

For the second half of the talk, write a note reading "I am the Way and the Truth and the Life. I am the only way to heaven," and place it in the Bible.

You will also need a Bible, a paper crown with the word *heaven* on it, and a picture of Jesus.

Gospel truth: Jesus is the only way to heaven. It is by His death and resurrection that we receive the crown of life.

Today we are going on a treasure hunt. At the end of the treasure hunt, we will all get something special to enjoy! But how will we find the treasure? We need some clues to help us. We need something to show the way. *Look in your pocket and find the first clue.* Oh, look! Maybe this note will help us find the way! *Read the clue and lead the children on the treasure hunt until they find the surprise waiting for them. When finished, return to the front.*

That was a great adventure! The notes we read gave us clues and showed us the way. At the end of the hunt, we found a treasure. There is another adventure that we are going on. It is a much longer adventure. It is a type of "treasure hunt" that we are on every day of our lives. At the end of *this* adventure we will find the most wonderful treasure of all—heaven! *Place the crown labeled* heaven *on a child's head.* We can call this treasure hunt a "heaven hunt."

How do we find the treasure called heaven? How do we find the way? *Hold up the Bible.* The answer to our questions is right here in the Bible. *Open the Bible, and read the second note.* This is an unusual clue! What does it mean? Who is the way to get to heaven? *Allow the children to respond.*

Hold up the picture of Jesus. Jesus is the way to heaven. He is telling us here that He is the *only* way to heaven. He died on the cross and rose again on the first Easter Sunday so we might all live forever with Him in heaven. He is also telling us that we can't find the treasure called heaven by ourselves. Jesus is the *only* way. Listen and see if you can count how many times we use the words *Jesus* and *heaven* in church today.

Prayer: Dear Jesus, You are the only way to heaven. Thank You for dying and rising again so that we may enjoy the treasures of heaven someday. In Your name we pray. Amen.

Seeing the Spirit in You

SIXTH SUNDAY OF EASTER: John 14:15–21

Text: "And I will ask the Father, and He will give you another Counselor to be with you forever—the Spirit of truth. The world cannot accept Him, because it neither sees Him nor knows Him. But you know Him, for He lives with you and will be in you." *John 14:16–17*

Teaching aids: A balloon and a permanent marker.

Gospel truth: Jesus is our Savior. God the Father has sent the Holy Spirit to us so that we might believe in Jesus. The Holy Spirit dwells in us and helps us live out the commands of Jesus.

A long time ago I learned that there was air all around. *Hold up your hands as if trying to touch the air.* I certainly can't feel the air. Can you? *Sniff.* I certainly can't smell the air. Can you? *Hold your hands above your eyes and peer all around.* I certainly can't see the air. Can you? Well, if you can't feel it or smell it or see it, how do you know there is air all around? Watch and I'll show you.

Begin to blow up the balloon. Do you know what is making the balloon get bigger? Yes, it's air. Air is filling the balloon. *Finish blowing up the balloon and knot it.* The more air I blow into the balloon, the bigger it gets. I can't actually see the air, but I can see what air can do.

There is something else around us and in us that we cannot see. That something else is called the Holy Spirit.

One day Jesus was talking to His disciples. He knew that

He was going to die and rise again. After His resurrection, Jesus knew He would be going back to heaven. He also knew that His disciples would miss Him and would need help remembering and believing in Him. So Jesus gave His disciples a promise. Jesus promised to ask God the Father to send the Holy Spirit to them. The Holy Spirit would help the disciples believe in Jesus and show their faith to others.

Jesus has given the same promise to us. We received the Holy Spirit when we were baptized. We cannot feel, smell, or see the Holy Spirit, but there is a way that we can know the Holy Spirit is alive in us.

Write the word love *on the balloon with the marker.* We said that we can look at the balloon to see what air can do. Well, we can look at the things we do and say to see what the Holy Spirit can do. The Holy Spirit helps us believe in Jesus. Jesus teaches us that people who believe in Him follow His commands to love one another. That means that every time we show the love of Jesus to each other, we are showing that the Holy Spirit is alive in us. The Holy Spirit helps us follow Jesus' example and love one another through the things we do and say.

How can you share Jesus' love with others? *Allow the children to answer.* When we do these things, we are following the commands of Jesus. When we do these things, we are showing that Jesus is alive in us. Because He died and rose again, someday we will all rejoice as we join Jesus and all believers in heaven. Until that day, the Holy Spirit is alive in us helping us show everyone around that we are alive in Jesus! Listen during the rest of the service and see how many times you hear the words *Holy Spirit, Jesus,* and *love.*

Prayer: Dear Jesus, thank You for the gift of the Holy Spirit. Help us show that the Holy Spirit is alive in us as we share Your love with others. In Your name we pray. Amen.

*Jesus*_____ *for Me*

SEVENTH SUNDAY OF EASTER: John 17:1–11

Text: "I will remain in the world no longer, but they are still in the world, and I am coming to You. Holy Father, protect them by the power of Your name—the name You gave Me—so that they may be one as We are one." *John 17:11*

Teaching aids: An 8″ × 36″ piece of poster board with the phrase "Jesus _____ for me" in large print. Also cut three smaller pieces of paper to fit in the blank—on one write "died"; on one write "lives"; and on the last write "prays." You will also need three clip clothespins.

Gospel truth: Even as Jesus died and lives for us, He also prays to God the Father on our behalf.

Ask two children to hold the poster board so the other children can see. Okay all you readers, get ready to read this message with me. As I point to each word, you read it out loud. *Point slowly to each word and read with the children,* Jesus (blank) for me.

Repeat a few times going faster and faster. Whoa! This doesn't make sense. Something is missing, and it belongs in the blank. It's like a mystery. Can you think of what the mystery word might be that would fit in the blank? *Allow the children to answer.*

You came up with some great ideas! Those are all words that could fit in the blank. Today we will look at three mystery words that will fit. Here's the first one. *Show the card with "died." Ask a child to cover the blank by attaching the card with a clothespin.* Let's read the new message together: Jesus *died* for me! Jesus loves us so much that He took our sins to the cross and died for each one of us!

Let's look at the second mystery word. *Ask another child to attach the card with "lives."* Let's read the second message together: Jesus *lives* for me. Jesus rose in victory over death and the grave. He lives for us today and every day so that we can live in Him.

You probably knew about those first two mystery words already. But this third mystery word might surprise you. *Ask another child to attach the card with "prays."* Let's read the third message together: Jesus *prays* for me. Did you know that? Did you know that Jesus loves you so much that He even prays to God the Father for you?

Listen to these words that Jesus prayed to God in our Bible reading today. "I pray for them. I am not praying for the world, but for those You have given Me, for they are Yours." Jesus is praying for His disciples and for you and for me. He knows that it is hard to be a believer in our world. There are people who might laugh at us for believing in Jesus or who might try to make us believe in something that they think is better than Jesus. But you know, and I know, that there is nothing better than being a believer in Jesus!

Point to each of the three cards. Yes, Jesus *died* for me. Jesus *lives* for me. And Jesus *prays* for me. Listen in the rest of the service for the words *Jesus* and *pray.* Jesus loves us very much, and that's no mystery!

Prayer: Dear Jesus, what a wonderful friend You are! You died for me! You live for me! And You pray for me! Help me stay true to You and follow You each and every day! In Your name we pray. Amen.

Same but Different

PENTECOST: John 16:5–11

Text: "But I tell you the truth: It is for your good that I am going away. Unless I go away, the Counselor will not come to you; but if I go, I will send Him to you." *John 16:7*

Teaching aids: Two frosted cupcakes on a plate or tray; three regular birthday candles and one "trick" birthday candle that will not blow out; matches and a glass of water for extinguishing the trick candle.

Gospel truth: We have received the Holy Spirit through Baptism and are set apart as believers, knowing that Jesus came to take away our sins and bring us salvation.

Ask an older child to hold the plate of cupcakes. Ask another child to hold the glass of water. Today is Pentecost—the birthday of the Christian church. We are going to celebrate with these two birthday cakes. All I need to do is add a birthday candle to each cupcake. *Add a regular candle to one cupcake and the trick candle to the other.*

There! Now each cupcake has a candle. They look the same don't they? They are both birthday candles, but even though they look the same, they are really quite different. Just watch. *Light the candles.* First I will blow out this candle. *Blow out the regular candle.* Now I will blow out the other candle. *Try to blow out the trick candle several times.*

Did you see that? The first candle blew out right away. The second candle didn't blow out at all. They looked the same, but they were quite different. *Extinguish the trick candle in water.*

The Bible tells us that *we* have something that makes us quite different from other people. We might look like everybody else—we might dress alike, talk alike, and even eat the same things—but God tells us that we are different. He made us different by giving the Holy Spirit to us. Now we don't have to be afraid of sin, death, and the devil. The Holy Spirit makes us alive as Jesus' people and He gives us faith. The Holy Spirit gives us the faith to believe that Jesus died for us and rose again. He helps us understand that our sins are forgiven for Jesus' sake. That is what makes us different!

Let's think about those candles again to learn one more thing about the Holy Spirit. Remember that even though each of these candles looks the same, they are really quite different. The first one can be blown out and the second one cannot. The second candle reminds me of the Holy Spirit. He will keep our faith burning inside of us, and He can never be blown away. He will always be with us.

Add the remaining candles to the cupcakes and light them. The Holy Spirit made us God's people when we were baptized. He is helping us celebrate the Church's birthday with all of God's children today. Let's sing happy birthday to our Church on its Pentecost birthday. *Lead the children in singing "Happy Birthday."* Listen for the words *Holy Spirit* and *Pentecost* in church today.

Prayer: Dear Father in heaven, Thank You for sending Your Holy Spirit to us. May the Holy Spirit keep our faith burning today and every day. In Jesus' name we pray. Amen.

One God, Father, Son, and Holy Spirit

THE HOLY TRINITY: Matt. 28:16–20

Text: "Therefore go and make disciples of all nations, baptizing them in the name of the Father and of the Son and of the Holy Spirit." *Matt. 28:19*

Teaching aid: A Bible and a bookmark made from three different-colored pieces of thick yarn braided together, which symbolizes the Holy Trinity. Place the bookmark in the Bible at Matt. 28:19.

Gospel truth: Jesus commands us to go out and make disciples, baptizing them in the name of the Father, the Son, and the Holy Spirit. Together we, as Jesus' disciples, celebrate our salvation in Him.

Gather the children around the baptismal font. If this is not possible, sit in a place where the children can see the baptismal font. Something wonderful happens at the baptismal font. Who knows what happens here? *Allow the children to respond.* Yes, we baptize people at the baptismal font. It is here that the Holy Spirit gives us faith and we become God's children.

But, *why* do we do that? Who told us to baptize people? That's right, Jesus did. We find His words right here in the Bible. *Open the Bible to Matthew 28 and read verse 19.* Jesus tells us to go make disciples and baptize them. We are to baptize people in God's name—in the name of the Father and of the Son and of the Holy Spirit.

One God (*hold up one finger*) with three names (*hold*

up three fingers). That's kind of confusing, isn't it? Maybe this Bible bookmark can help us understand. It is one bookmark made from three strands of yarn. *Take the braided bookmark apart but do not separate the three strands entirely.* The three different colors help us see the three different strands of yarn. *Name the three colors as you separate the strands.* But it is not three bookmarks; it is one bookmark.

The same thing is true about God. We baptize in the name of God the Father, God the Son, and God the Holy Spirit. God is not three Gods (*hold up three fingers*) but one God (*hold up one finger*). *Point to one strand of yarn.* God the Father created us and the whole world. He leads, protects, and guides us. *Point to the second strand of yarn.* God the Son redeemed us. He led a perfect life with no sin, then took our sins to the cross when He died for us. He rose again in victory so that we might live in heaven forever. *Point to the third strand of yarn.* God the Holy Spirit works faith in us so that we can believe that God the Father made us and that Jesus, God's Son, redeemed us. *Braid the strands together again.* Three colors but one bookmark. Three names but one God.

Listen carefully the next time there is a Baptism. Listen for the names of God the Father, God the Son, and God the Holy Spirit. Think about how God is three in one. Ask the Holy Spirit to help you follow Jesus' command and tell everyone about your loving God—Father, Son, and Holy Spirit.

Prayer: God the Father, God the Son, and God the Holy Spirit, Three in One. Guide and keep us every day, walking with you all the way. In Jesus' name we pray. Amen.

Thumbs Up!

—➤◆◄—

SECOND SUNDAY AFTER PENTECOST:
Matt. 7:21–29

Text: "Therefore everyone who hears these words of Mine and puts them into practice is like a wise man who built his house on the rock." *Matt. 7:24*

Teaching aid: A Bible, a paper plate with a happy face drawn on it, and a paper plate with a sad face drawn on it.

Gospel truth: Jesus helps us listen to His words and put them into practice. Firmly rooted in His Word, we are like the wise man who built his house on a rock.

In today's Gospel lesson, Jesus tells His disciples about a foolish man (*hold up the sad face and give a "thumbs down" sign*) and a wise man (*hold up the happy face and give a "thumbs up" sign*).

Let's practice your "thumbs up" and "thumbs down" signs. When I hold up the sad face, you give me a "thumbs down" sign. When I hold up the happy face, you give me a "thumbs up" sign. *Repeat this activity several times.* Now you are ready. As I tell you the story, watch the faces to see when to give me a "thumbs up" or a "thumbs down" sign.

Jesus is talking to His disciples and telling them to be very careful. The disciples have been with Him for a long time and have been listening to all that He has taught them. Now that's a wise, (*hold up the happy face*) "thumbs up" thing to do.

But Jesus tells His friends to be careful because other people who do not believe in Him will try to make the disciples forget Jesus' words and turn away from Him. Now, that would be a foolish (*hold up the sad face*) "thumbs down" thing to do. In fact, Jesus says that the only way to keep those (*sad face*) "thumbs down" people away is to keep remembering the words of Jesus and doing them. Then it will be (*happy face*) "thumbs up" all the way.

Jesus goes on to tell His disciples that people who do not listen to His words and do them are like a foolish man (*sad face*) who built his house on sand. The house looked great, but when the rain and the winds came, the house fell down. What a foolish (*sad face*) thing to do.

People who do not listen to the words of Jesus are like that foolish man. They may do things that look good and act the way they think they are supposed to, but when temptations come, they make the wrong choices because they are not paying attention to the words of Jesus (*sad face*). Then lots of things start to crumble around them.

Jesus tells us to be like the wise man (*happy face*) who built his house on a rock. The house looked great, and when the winds and the rains came, the house stayed standing. What a wise (*happy face*) place to build a house.

People who listen carefully to Jesus' words and follow Him are like that wise man. When temptations come, Jesus helps them make the right choices and God's Holy Spirit makes their faith stronger and stronger and stronger (*happy face*).

You and I can be like the foolish man (*sad face*) or the wise man (*happy face*). We have the words of Jesus right here in the Bible. *Hold up the Bible.* We can listen to His words, learn them, and remember them. We can look to the words of Jesus to help us make the right choices.

For example, when someone tries to tell us that we should skip church or Sunday school and play baseball instead (*sad face*), we can listen to the words of Jesus and make the wise choice. We can go to church first and play baseball later (*happy face*). Or when others try to tell us to make fun of someone else (*sad face*), we can make the wise choice and be a friend instead (*happy face*).

Jesus' Word and the Holy Spirit in our hearts help us be "thumbs up" all the way! Listen for the words *foolish, wise, sand,* and *rock* in the service today.

Prayer: Dear Jesus, it is difficult to know how to make the wise choices that are part of following You. Help us stay firmly rooted in Your Word and send Your Holy Spirit to keep the faith in our hearts strong. In Your name we pray. Amen.

Big and Small, He Came for Us All

THIRD SUNDAY AFTER PENTECOST:
Matt. 9:9–13

Text: "But go and learn what this means: 'I desire mercy, not sacrifice.' For I have not come to call the righteous, but sinners." *Matt. 9:13*

Teaching aid: Something bulky and/or slightly heavy (like a chair or a big box) that can be moved from one place to another.

Gospel truth: Jesus came for all sinners and He calls each one to follow Him.

Set the bulky item slightly in the way where the children will be sitting so that it will have to be moved. Sit partially behind it so that you cannot see everyone. Hello. It's good to see all of you here today. Well, I really can't see everyone. This thing is in the way. I guess I will need someone to help me move it. *Instead of choosing the oldest and/or biggest child, choose two or three of the younger and/or smaller children to help you. Move the bulky item over to one side.*

That's better. Now I can see everyone! I noticed that a lot of you wanted to volunteer to help me move that big thing out of the way. You probably thought your strong muscles were the best for moving it. You were probably surprised when I chose some smaller children to be my helpers instead of you. Maybe you even thought that you would have made a better helper than the ones I chose. In fact, some of you probably thought you could even move the whole thing all by yourself! Well, I know that *all* of you would have been great helpers, but I chose the smaller children in order to teach you about something that Jesus says in today's Gospel lesson.

Jesus chose some special helpers, the disciples, to be with Him and learn from Him. One day He chose someone to be a disciple that surprised a lot of people. Jesus chose a man named Matthew, who was a tax collector. Most people did not like tax collectors because they thought the tax collectors were cheating them out of their money. Some people even called tax collectors "sinners," thinking that the tax collectors' sins were worse than their own.

After choosing Matthew as a disciple, Jesus ate supper with him and some of his friends. Some people called Pharisees watched them. The Pharisees thought that they were better than the tax collectors. They couldn't understand why Jesus would choose these "sinners" to be His special helpers. Jesus told the Pharisees that He did not come to this world for people who think that they are better than others or who think they do not need Him. Instead, He came for the people who know they are sinners and let the Holy Spirit lead them to be His followers.

We know that we need Jesus. We are sinners and cannot get to heaven by ourselves. We know that Jesus died for us and rose again and that He lives for us. We are like Matthew, the tax collector, and all of his "sinner" friends. Jesus calls *all* of us, young and old and weak and strong, to be His followers. Listen for the words *Matthew, sin, follow,* and *save* today. Remember that each one of us is special to Jesus. He has chosen us to follow Him.

Prayer: Dear Jesus, thank You for coming into the world for sinners like us. Help us each day to follow You and remember that You are our Savior, helper, and friend. In Your name we pray. Amen.

Linked Together in His Love

———◆———

FOURTH SUNDAY AFTER PENTECOST:
Matt. 9:35–10:8

Text: "Ask the Lord of the harvest, therefore, to send out workers into His harvest field." *Matt. 9:38*

Teaching aid: A chain with links (a bicycle chain, chain leash, tire chain, etc.); a paper chain made of 12 8″ × 2″ strips of paper with the name of one of Jesus' disciples written on each strip; several more 8″ × 2″ paper strips. You'll also need markers and a stapler. You may want to recruit another adult to help you with this message.

Gospel truth: We are all disciples of Jesus sent out into the world to share the Gospel message of Jesus' death and resurrection with others. We are strongly linked together through our saving faith, yet we are sent out individually as well as together.

Have you ever looked closely at a chain? Let's look at this one. *Hold up the real chain for all to see.* A chain is made of individual pieces that are linked together. These links make the chain strong. When one is pulled, the other parts of the chain work together to keep it strong.

Hold up the paper chain. Here is a different type of chain made of paper. It's strong in a different way. The strength of this chain has to do with the names that are written on each strip of paper. Let's read the names on the chain. *Read the disciples' names.* These are the names of the 12 disciples Jesus called to be His special helpers. They were linked together in Jesus' love and strong in their trust and faith in Him.

Tear the first strip off of the chain. Jesus called Andrew to help Him share God's love with others. *Add more links to the chain.* Now more believers were linked together in Jesus' love. Then Jesus called Peter (add more links to the chain) to tell others the good news. Even more believers were linked together. *Continue to make links and staple them to the chain.* As Jesus' disciples helped Him, more and more people were linked together in God's love. *Hold up the long chain.*

There are still many more people today who need to hear the Good News about Jesus. You and I are the special helpers that Jesus is sending out now. *Write some of the children's names on paper strips.* He is sending out (*name one of the children and add a link to the chain*) to share the Good News with others. *Continue with other children as time allows.*

Jesus sends all of us who believe in Him to share the Good News with others. We are all linked together in the trust and faith God's Holy Spirit gives us in Jesus. *Hold up the long paper chain.* One day, because Jesus died and rose for us, we will be together in heaven.

Prayer: Dear Jesus, You have given us a big job to share the message of Your love with others. Help us remember that You do not ask us to do this task alone. We are linked together with You and all other believers so that, together, we will be strong. In Your name we pray. Amen.

Something to Shout About

FIFTH SUNDAY AFTER PENTECOST:
Matt. 10:24–33

Text: "What I tell you in the dark, speak in the daylight; what is whispered in your ear, proclaim from the roofs. ... Whoever acknowledges Me before men, I will also acknowledge him before My Father in heaven." *Matt. 10:27, 32.*

Teaching aid: A radio or an audiocassette player and an audiocassette of music; a piece of poster board with "Jesus Is My Savior" printed in very large letters.

Gospel truth: The message of salvation is not to be whispered, but it is to be shouted and proclaimed! When we acknowledge Jesus before others, He acknowledges us before God, our Father in heaven.

Before the service, turn the volume of the radio or audiocassette player very low so that the music can barely be heard. Hello, boys and girls! I'd like to share some of my favorite music with you today. *Hold the radio or player close to your ear. Move to the music and hum along.*

What's the matter? How come none of you are moving to the beat? It's a great song! What? You can't hear it? Well, no wonder you weren't responding! Here, let me turn it a little louder so that you all can hear! *Turn the volume louder and invite the children to move in rhythm.*

Do you know that you have just reminded me of something very important? If I have something that I want to share with you, I need to be sure that you can hear it! For example, how can you enjoy my favorite music if you can't hear it?

I just thought of some exciting news that I would like to share with you. *Whisper something like, "I have a new puppy," in the ear of the person sitting next to you. Look at the others with an excited look.* Isn't that exciting? I'm so excited I can hardly stand it!

Look around. What's the matter? Why aren't you excited with me? What? You didn't hear my exciting news? Let me tell you again. This time I won't whisper, but I will shout out loud. *Repeat the good news and lead the children in a cheer.* You did it once again, boys and girls! You reminded me that I should not keep exciting news a secret! I need to shout it out loud so that you can be excited with me!

Jesus reminds us to speak His Good News loudly in our Gospel lesson today. Jesus tells us that we are to speak aloud the Good News that He died and rose for us, and we are to proclaim it from the rooftops. The news that Jesus is our Savior is better than any favorite song and even better than (*a new puppy*)! We are to let *everybody, everywhere* know that Jesus is our friend and Savior. Jesus even tells us that we will be blessed when we acknowledge Him as our friend and Savior.

Let's practice sharing the Good News of Jesus! *Hold up the poster and read it with the children.* Let's shout this message to everyone sitting in the church—all our moms and dads and brothers and sisters and grandpas and grandmas need to hear this Good News! *Shout the message together. If necessary, try it a second time a little louder.* Now, go out and tell everyone you meet the good news of the Gospel! Claim Jesus as your Savior and friend because He is the best friend we can ever have!

Prayer: Dear Jesus, You are a wonderful friend and a loving Savior. Help us share this Good News with everyone in a joyful, proclaiming way! In Your name we pray. Amen.

Perfect, Unwrinkled Love

—————◆—————

SIXTH SUNDAY AFTER PENTECOST:
Matt. 10:34–42

Text: "Anyone who loves his father or mother more than Me is not worthy of Me; anyone who loves his son or daughter more than Me is not worthy of Me; and anyone who does not take his cross and follow Me is not worthy of Me. Whoever finds his life will lose it, and whoever loses his life for My sake will find it." *Matt. 10:37–39*

Teaching aid: Two hearts cut from red paper; scissors.

Gospel truth: Being a disciple of Jesus is not easy. There will be quarrels, anger, and even hate. But Jesus forgives us, keeps us close to Him, and leads us to heaven.

Hold up a heart. Do you know what I think of when I see this heart? *Allow the children to answer.* Actually, I think of two things. I think of love and I think of you. Whenever I see a heart I think of all the love we have to share with each other. I know that each one of you is really good at doing loving things for each other. What are some ways you can show love to each other? *Allow the children to respond.*

Those are all great ideas! There are so many loving, kind things we can do for each other. Jesus tells us that even the smallest things, like giving a drink of cold water to a little child, are really big things if they are done with His love in our hearts. But people don't always act kind and loving, do they? *Begin to crumple the heart.* Sometimes friends fight with each other. Sometimes even families fight. Sometimes people think other things are more important than Jesus. *Crumple the heart some more.*

Open up the crumpled heart. Look what's happened to our heart—it's all wrinkled! *Try to straighten out the wrinkles.* And no matter what we try to do, we cannot take out the wrinkles by ourselves.

Cut a cross from the wrinkled heart. That's why Jesus came into our world. He brought God's perfect love to us. He showed that perfect, unwrinkled love to us when He died on the cross and rose again. Because of His perfect love, He forgives all of us for all the times that we fail to show His love. He smooths out the wrinkles in our hearts. *Hold up the other, unwrinkled heart.* He helps us be His disciples. He helps us remember that He is the most important thing in our lives. And He helps us through all the wrinkled, troubled times we have on earth until it is time for us to live with Him in heaven. Listen for the words *love* and *cross* in church today.

Prayer: Dear Jesus, You have called us to be Your disciples and to share the example of Your love with others. Help us know that we are forgiven for the times when we think other things are more important than You. Help us know that You are with us to lead us so that we might be examples of Your love to others. In Your name we pray. Amen.

Sharing the Heavy Load

SEVENTH SUNDAY AFTER PENTECOST: Matt. 11:25–30

Text: "Come to Me, all you who are weary and burdened, and I will give you rest. Take My yoke upon you and learn from Me, for I am gentle and humble in heart, and you will find rest for your souls. For My yoke is easy and My burden is light." *Matt. 11:28–30*

Teaching aid: A long piece of plywood that's too cumbersome for one person to carry; 3" × 5" pieces of paper or index cards; markers; tape.

Gospel truth: Jesus tells us to bring our burdens to Him and He will give us rest. He has given the reassurance of salvation to us, and He will share in our burdens while we are here on earth.

Lay the piece of plywood on the floor in front of the children. Look at this long, long board. I think I will pick it up and carry it all by myself. *Pick up the plywood in the center and make it wobble back and forth.*

Whoa! This is too much for me to handle by myself! What should I do? *Allow the children to respond.* You're right! I'll choose someone to help me carry this. *Ask a volunteer to hold one end while you move down to hold the other.* Wow! This is much better! It's easier to carry a big load when there is someone to share it with you! *Set the plywood back on the floor.*

There are lots of things in our lives that are hard to handle by ourselves, like things that we worry about or things that make us afraid. What makes you worry? What makes you afraid? *Write some of the answers on the paper or index cards. Ask some children to tape these to the plywood. Answers might include illness, parents without jobs, being alone, taking a test, moving to a new house, quarrels in the family, not having friends, etc.*

These things can make us feel worried, frightened, and afraid. Jesus calls them "burdens," and He knows all about them. *Try to pick up the plywood by yourself again.* Just like this board was hard for me to carry by myself, Jesus knows that our worries and troubles are hard to carry. We get tired and weary when we try to carry them by ourselves.

Ask another person to help you carry the plywood. Just like this board is easier to carry when I share the load, Jesus says our burdens will be easier to carry because He has promised to help us. He says, "Come to Me, all you who are weary and burdened, and I will give you rest."

Jesus loves us so much that He died for us to take away the burden of our sin. Because He rose again, one day we will live with Him in heaven where there are no worries or burdens. Until then, Jesus invites us to bring our troubles to Him so that He can help us carry the heavy load. Listen for the words *burden* and *light* and the phrase "come to Me" in church today.

Prayer: Dear Jesus, You know what makes us worried, anxious, and afraid, even before we do. Help us remember that You are there to share our burdens with us. You are there to help us carry the heavy load. Thank You, Jesus. In Your name we pray. Amen.

The Little Seeds That Grow and Grow

≫•≪

EIGHTH SUNDAY AFTER PENTECOST:
Matt. 13:1–9

Text: "Still other seed fell on good soil, where it produced a
crop—a hundred, sixty or thirty times what was sown.
He who has ears, let him hear." *Matt. 13:8–9*

Teaching aid: Fold four cards, each with a sunflower seed
(or other large seed) glued on the inside. On the front of
the first card, print "Birds"; on the front of the second
card, print "Rocks"; on the front of the third card, print
"Thorns"; and on the front of the fourth card, draw a
large, healthy green plant. Before beginning the message, fold the front of each card so the children see the
seed first.

Gospel truth: God sows the seed of the Gospel, His Word.
Some people close their hearts to God's Word so the
seeds of faith wither and die. God's Holy Spirit helps us
respond to God's Word so that the seeds grow into faith
that can be nourished and shared with others.

*Hold all four cards in your hand with the seeds facing
the children.* Today I will tell you a story about a farmer who
planted seeds in four different places. *Show the first card.*
The first seed was thrown on the ground, but (*close the flap*)
birds came along and ate it. No plant grew there.
Show the second card. The second seed fell on rocky

ground. It began to grow, but the roots couldn't reach very far down into the ground because they ran into rocks. *Close the flap.* When the hot sun came out, the small plant withered and died. No plant grew there.

Show the third card. The third seed sent roots down into the soil and began to grow. But soon weeds and thorns (*close the flap*) grew around it and took all the nourishment from the soil. They choked the plant and it died.

Show the fourth card. Finally, the farmer planted seed in good soil. The seed sent roots far down into the ground. The seed got lots of sunshine and rain and plenty of nourishment. *Close the flap.* And guess what! The little seed grew and grew! It grew into healthy plants with lots of good food to eat.

This is not a story I made up. This is a story Jesus told us. He wants us to know that the seed is like God's Word. Sometimes when people hear God's Word, other things get in the way and keep them from believing that Jesus died and rose for them. Maybe these people wouldn't care enough about Jesus to come to church, or pray, or read their Bibles. Maybe they would think that other things were more important than Jesus. Their faith would never be able to grow, just like the seeds in our story.

But God's Holy Spirit plants the seed of God's Word in our hearts. He helps our faith in Jesus grow and grow. The Holy Spirit makes us excited about Jesus and helps us feed our faith when we come to church, pray, sing songs of praise to God, and read the Bible. Listen for the words *seed* and *grow* in church today.

Prayer: Dear Jesus, thank You for helping the seeds of faith grow in our hearts every day. Give us the Holy Spirit to feed our faith and keep it growing so that we might share our faith with others. In Your name we pray. Amen.

Watch Out for Those Weeds!

Text: "Let both grow together until the harvest. At that time I will tell the harvesters: First collect the weeds and tie them in bundles to be burned; then gather the wheat and bring it into my barn." *Matt. 13:30*

Teaching aid: Use the fourth card from the children's message for the Eighth Sunday after Pentecost. Also bring a large, healthy potted plant.

Gospel truth: God's Holy Spirit keeps our faith strong so that we will enter the kingdom of heaven at the time of harvest.

Hold up the seed card from last Sunday's message. Do you remember the story of the little seed that grew and grew? We said that the plant that grew from that little seed was like your faith in Jesus. God's Holy Spirit will keep it growing day after day!

Hold up the potted plant. Look at what we have here—a healthy plant that keeps on growing! A long time ago, seeds were planted into good ground and, with proper care, the little plant has grown into a very big plant.

But some days I really worried whether it would grow! Every once in awhile a weed would pop up around the plant and start to take away the good nourishment in the soil. That happens to plants sometimes. It's difficult for a plant to grow with weeds all around. It has to dig its roots way down deep into the soil, and it has to try hard to get as much rain and sunshine as possible.

Let's imagine that this plant is your faith. It was planted through the seed of God's Word when you were baptized. The Holy Spirit helps it to grow every day. But watch out for the weeds around you! The weeds are people who do not believe in Jesus. Those weeds might be friends or family members who do not love Jesus and who try to get you to stop believing in Him. Those weeds might be people at school or in your neighborhood who say believing in Jesus is silly.

God gives us His Holy Spirit to keep our faith strong. He won't let people who don't love Him destroy our faith. He helps us grow by putting us in His church and Sunday school and with our families. Jesus is on our side helping our faith grow. Jesus died for us and rose again to win us new life. He is stronger than any weed that wants to destroy our faith! Some day all of those weeds will die and be thrown away, while all people who believe in Jesus as their Savior will enter the kingdom of heaven. Listen for the words *seed*, *weed*, and *heaven* in church today. And thank God for protecting your faith from weeds!

Prayer: Dear God, it makes us sad to know that there are people who don't believe in You. Help us to tell those people about You. Keep our faith strong so that we might rejoice in heaven someday! In Jesus' name we pray. Amen.

A Special Treasure

⤜➤◆◆⬤◄⤛

TENTH SUNDAY AFTER PENTECOST:
Matt. 13:44–52

Text: "The kingdom of heaven is like treasure hidden in a field. When a man found it, he hid it again, and then in his joy went and sold all he had and bought that field. Again, the kingdom of heaven is like a merchant looking for fine pearls. When he found one of great value, he went away and sold everything he had and bought it." *Matt 13:44–46*

Teaching aid: Glass cake pan (9″ × 13″ or larger), filled with dirt; large pearl or round white bead; a child's toy that is currently popular. The toy should be small enough to bury in the pan. Also have a small cardboard cross for each child. (You may want to spray-paint the crosses gold or cut them from gold poster board.) You also will need something to hold the crosses until you hand them out.

Gospel truth: Life in heaven with Jesus is more special than anything we can buy, find, or have on earth.

Have you ever found something that was really special? Have you ever wanted anything so much that you were ready to trade it for everything else that you have? *Show the pan of dirt in which you have buried a currently popular toy.* What if I told you that you might find something really special in my pan of dirt this morning? Would you look for it? *Ask one or two children to "dig" for the treasure.* But there's a problem. You found this treasure in *my* dirt, so it belongs to me. You can't just take it. You need to buy it from me. What will you do?

Ask the children to respond. Those are all good suggestions, but my price is pretty steep for this treasure. You will need to sell *all* of your toys to have enough money to buy this treasure. Who still wants to buy my treasure?

In our Gospel lesson today, Jesus tells us that there is something that is so special that anybody who finds it, knows it as the most important thing ever. Can anyone guess what that might be? *Allow the children to answer. Accept all answers.* Jesus doesn't just make us guess what the answer might be. He tells us!

In the Bible reading today, Jesus tells us that heaven is that special thing that is the best treasure ever. He says, "The kingdom of heaven is like treasure hidden in a field. When a man found it, he hid it again, and then in his joy went and sold all he had and bought that field. Again, the kingdom of heaven is like a merchant looking for fine pearls. When he found one of great value, he went away and sold everything he had and bought it."

Show the children the pearl. The man in the story thought the pearl was a wonderful treasure. But Jesus is telling us that heaven is more special than any of the good things He gives us to enjoy. It's better than the best toy you can have. It's better than the best house your mom and dad could buy. It's better than the best car you can ride in. It's better than the fanciest clothes. In heaven, we will be with Jesus forever.

Do you know what the best part is? We don't have to buy heaven. Jesus gives it to us! He died for our sins so that we can be forgiven and one day live with Him in heaven. Because God's Holy Spirit gives us faith in Him, He will take us to heaven when we die. Isn't that great?

During the rest of the worship service today, there are two special words I want you to listen for. They are *Jesus* and *heaven.* Listen to see how many times you hear them.

Let's pray together. *Use the prayer below or lead the children in thanking God for His gifts of faith and heaven.*

As you go back to your seats, I have a golden cross to help you remember that heaven is a special treasure that Jesus gives to each of us. Take it with you and tell a grown-up today that Jesus loves us and wants us to be in heaven with Him someday.

Prayer: Dear Jesus, we're so glad that You died for us and want us to live with You in heaven. Thank You for this special treasure. Help us tell others about You and about Your special gift of heaven for us. In Your name we pray. Amen.

Loaves
and Fishes

━━◆━━

ELEVENTH SUNDAY AFTER PENTECOST:
Matt. 14:13–21

Text: Taking the five loaves and the two fish and looking up
to heaven, He gave thanks and broke the loaves. Then
He gave them to the disciples, and the disciples gave
them to the people. They all ate and were satisfied, and
the disciples picked up twelve basketfuls of broken
pieces that were left over. *Matt. 14:19–20*

Teaching aid: Small loaf of bread, unsliced, and a medium-
sized basket, preferably a wicker basket with a cover.

Gospel truth: Jesus takes care of all our needs. He knows
and cares when we are hungry or when we need anything that He can give us.

Hold up the bread. Can anyone tell me what this is? Of
course you can. It's a loaf of bread. In today's Gospel lesson,
Jesus uses a loaf of bread to do something special. Listen
while I tell the story.

One day Jesus was teaching and talking to a very large
crowd of people. Can any of you count to 5,000? The Bible
tells us that Jesus was teaching a group of 5,000 men, and
that there were women and children besides that. That
means there might have been 15,000 or more people all
together. That's a lot, isn't it?

Jesus told the people about God and how much He
loved them. He talked so long that it started to get dark. The
disciples started to get worried because nobody had any

food to feed all these people. They asked Jesus to send the people to the town to get food.

But Jesus said, "The people don't have to buy food. You can give them something to eat." Now the disciples were really worried! They knew they didn't have enough food for that many people.

Show the basket. Do you think I could put enough food in this basket to feed everybody who is here in church this morning? You're right. It's not big enough.

In the Bible story we're talking about today, the disciples had only five loaves of bread and two small fish to use to feed everyone. They brought those to Jesus, but they were worried. They didn't think that would be enough food. But Jesus took that small amount of food, gave thanks to God for it, and broke the bread and the fish into small pieces. Let's do that right now. Let's look up to heaven and say, "Thank You, God." Say it with me, all together.

Now do you think this will be enough to feed everybody here? Could I feed you with it? Could I feed all the grown-ups? There might be enough for all of us sitting right here, but I think I'd run out of bread before I could feed all the grown-ups.

But that's not what happened when Jesus did it. If you know this story, you know that Jesus and the disciples fed all those people—all of the men, all of the women, and all of the children—and there was still bread left over. Jesus told the disciples to take their empty lunch baskets and pick up all the crumbs and all the leftovers. Do you think the disciples were surprised to fill all their baskets with leftovers? I think they were surprised.

Jesus did something on that day that only God can do. We call it a miracle because He took that little bit of food and fed that big, big crowd of people with it. That's a miracle that only God can do.

Jesus takes care of us just like that. He cares about us and knows everything that we need. He gives us grown-ups to take care of us and make sure we have what we need.

Let's thank Jesus for taking care of us. *Lead the children in the prayer below or in a prayer of your own. You may want to use the prayer as an echo prayer. Say one phrase and ask the children to repeat it.*

In church today, there are three words I'd like you to listen for. I think you might even be able to guess what they are. They are *loaves* and *fish* and *Jesus*. Listen and count how many times you hear them.

Now as you go back to your seats, I'm going to break off a piece of this bread to give to you. Be sure to tell a friend or a grown-up about the special time when Jesus used bread like this to feed lots and lots of people. Ask your mom or dad if you can eat this bread after you tell the story.

Prayer: Dear Jesus, thank You for taking care of us. Be with us today and every day. Help us tell others about You and how special You are. In Your name we pray. Amen.

Don't Be Afraid

─━◆━─

TWELFTH SUNDAY AFTER PENTECOST:
Matt. 14:22–33

Text: When the disciples saw Him walking on the lake, they were terrified. "It's a ghost," they said, and cried out in fear. But Jesus immediately said to them: "Take courage! It is I. Don't be afraid." *Matt. 14:26–27*

Teaching aid: Large bowl with water; two small (3″ or 4″) plastic figures of people; one small boat. *Optional:* Small plastic boats to hand out to the children.

Gospel truth: Jesus will always be with us and help us when we are afraid.

How many of you like to walk in puddles? What happens if the puddle is really deep? What happens when you try to walk on top of water that's really deep? Do your feet stay on top of the water or do they go under the water?

Today I want to tell you a story about a time when Jesus walked on water. That's pretty amazing, isn't it?

After Jesus had fed all those people with the five loaves and two fish that we heard about last Sunday, He told the disciples to go out on the lake in their boat. He told them He would meet them later on the other side of the lake. *Put the bowl of water in your lap. Place the small boat in the water at one edge.*

So the disciples got into the boat and sailed off. *If your boat is sturdy enough to hold one of the people figures, place one figure in the boat. Push the boat as if it is sail-*

ing. It was a windy night, and it took a long time to sail to the other side. *Use your hand to make the water churn as if it were windy.*

When it was very late, Jesus decided to go out to meet His disciples. But He didn't use a boat. He just stepped out on the lake and started to walk on top of the water. WOW! We couldn't do that, could we? *Hold the second figure so that it "walks" on the water.*

Meanwhile, the disciples were working hard to steer the boat to the other side of the lake. When they saw someone walking on the water, they couldn't believe their eyes. They didn't know it was Jesus. They thought it was a ghost. They were scared.

But Jesus knew they were scared. "Don't be afraid," He said. "It is I, Jesus."

The disciples were surprised! Peter said, "Jesus, if it's really You, tell me to walk to You on the water." And Jesus told him to come.

Take the figure out of the boat and "walk" it toward Jesus. Peter got out of the boat and started to walk. Do you know what? His feet stayed on top of the water, just like Jesus! Just then, the wind blew harder. Peter looked around him at the big waves and he got scared. As soon as he got scared, he started to sink. *Let the figure begin to sink into the water.*

Peter called out to Jesus. "Help," he said. "Save me!" Jesus reached out and took Peter's hand and helped him walk over to the boat. *"Walk" the two figures to the boat.* As they climbed into the boat, all the disciples knew it was Jesus, and they thanked Him for saving Peter. "You really are God," they said. And they weren't afraid anymore.

Have you ever been afraid—maybe of a loud noise or of thunder or of the dark? When you're afraid, what do you do? Some of you probably call out to Mom or Dad to come and make you feel safe, don't you? Do you ever think about Jesus when you're scared? Do you ever pray for Jesus to help you feel safe? That's a good thing to do!

Let's pray together to ask Jesus to help us remember to pray to Him when we're scared. *Lead the children in the prayer below or use your own prayer based on answers the children have given during the message.*

In church today, there are some special words to listen for. The first words go together—"Don't be afraid." Do you remember who said those words in the story? *Allow the children to answer.* That's right, it was Jesus. And that's the other word I want you to listen for—*Jesus.* He helps us when we are afraid.

As you go back to your seats, I want to give you a small boat to take back with you. You can use it to tell the story of Jesus walking on the water. You might even want to put some water in the sink to tell your story. I know you'll want to tell it to a friend or a grown-up today. Have a good day, and remember that Jesus loves you.

Prayer: Dear Jesus, thank You for taking care of me. Help me remember that when I'm afraid, I can talk to You. In Your name I pray. Amen.

Jesus
Heals Us

THIRTEENTH SUNDAY AFTER PENTECOST:
Matt. 15:21–28

Text: Then Jesus answered, "Woman, you have great faith! Your request is granted." And her daughter was healed from that very hour. *Matt. 15:28*

Teaching aid: Large bandage, splint, or cast for a broken bone; a small adhesive bandage for each child.

Gospel truth: Jesus cares for us when we are sick. Best of all, He heals our spirits by forgiving our sins.

How many of you have ever worn one of these? *Show the splint or bandage you have brought.* Why do people use this? Do you think it's fun to wear? I don't! We wear one of these only when we have a broken bone or are hurt badly.

In the Gospel lesson today, a woman asked Jesus to heal her daughter. In fact, she asked and asked and asked. Even when the disciples wanted to send her away, she kept on asking. And she kept on believing that Jesus would heal her daughter.

Jesus said, "Woman, you have great faith!" And He told her that her daughter would be healed. Jesus didn't even need to use a bandage (splint/cast) like this to heal her daughter. Wow! That's another miracle!

Remember last Sunday when we talked about the storm and about Jesus walking on the water? That was a miracle too. Miracles are special things that only God can do. Jesus did miracles to show the people that He really *was* God's Son.

Today Jesus heals people who are sick through doctors and bandages and medicine. But there's another kind of sickness that I want to tell you about. It's the sickness we call sin. It causes all the bad things we do. Jesus heals sin too.

Jesus came to earth to die for us and take away our sins. Then He rose again on Easter to win us new life with Him. Jesus not only helps our bodies get better—He also heals our souls from sin.

Let's thank Jesus for being so good to us. *Use the prayer below or a prayer of your own. Ask the children to repeat each phrase after you.*

Listen for two special words in church today. If you hold up two fingers, you can put a word on each finger to help you remember. The words are *healing* and *Jesus.* Count how many times you hear them today.

As you go back to your seats, I have a special reminder about today's Gospel lesson. You can use it to tell someone how great Jesus is and how He heals our sins. It's a bandage. The next time Mom or Dad puts one of these on a scratch, remember the healing inside that Jesus does for each of us as He takes away our sins. *Give each child a bandage.*

Prayer: Dear Jesus, thank You for taking care of us when we are sick. Thank You for dying on the cross to take away our sins. Thank You for healing our souls from sin. Help us tell others how great You are. In Your name we pray. Amen.

Big Rock, Little Rocks

FOURTEENTH SUNDAY AFTER PENTECOST: Matt. 16:13–20

Text: Simon Peter answered, "You are the Christ, the Son of the living God." Jesus replied, "… you are Peter, and on this rock I will build My church." *Matt. 16:16, 18*

Teaching aid: Large stone; small stone for each child.

Gospel truth: Jesus is our Savior. God's Holy Spirit gives us faith in Him that is as solid and firm as a rock.

Hold up the large rock. What am I holding? That's right. It's a rock. Do you think it's heavy or light? Right again. It's heavy!

Sometimes we talk about a rock like this as being a "solid rock." Why do you think we say that? *Allow the children to answer.* Do you think this rock would be easy or hard to break? Is it easy or hard to lift? to move? Right. This rock is hard to break, hard to lift, and hard to move. That's why people might call it a solid rock.

In the Gospel lesson today, Jesus calls our faith in Him a solid rock. He says that His church (the people who believe in Him) is built on the solid rock of faith in Jesus and His payment for our sins on the cross.

Jesus also tells Peter that he is like a little rock or pebble. In fact, Peter's name means "little rock" or "pebble." *Show one of the small stones.* Even though this little rock is small, it still is very hard to break. Jesus tells Peter that he is like that little rock because he believes in Jesus. Each of us is like this little rock because we believe in Jesus. God's Holy Spirit keeps our faith in Jesus strong and hard to break.

Let's thank Jesus for making us strong like a rock. Let's hold hands as we pray. That will help us remember that we are even stronger together than we are all alone. *Lead the children in the prayer below or in a prayer of your own.*

Listen for three words today. Hold up three fingers and pretend you are putting a word on each finger to help you remember them. The words today are *Jesus* and *Peter* and *rock.* Say them with me to help you remember—*Jesus. Peter. Rock.*

As you go back to your seats, I'm going to give you each a little rock. You can put your little rock in a special place to help you remember that Jesus keeps your faith in Him strong. Be sure to tell someone why your little rock is so special.

Prayer: Dear Jesus, thank You for dying on the cross and taking away our sins. Thank You for keeping our faith strong like little rocks. In Your name we pray. Amen.

Carrying a Cross

FIFTEENTH SUNDAY AFTER PENTECOST:
Matt. 16:21–26

Text: Then Jesus said to His disciples, "If anyone would come after Me, he must deny himself and take up his cross and follow Me." *Matt. 16:24*

Teaching aid: Large wall cross; small cross for each child. *Optional:* Give each child a second cross to share with a friend.

Gospel truth: We will have problems and troubles as we follow Jesus, but He promises to love and care for us.

Hold up the large cross. Who can tell me what this is? That's right, it's a cross. Why is the cross important? *Allow the children to answer.* Right again. The cross is important because it helps us remember that Jesus loves us so much that He died on the cross to take away our sins.

In the Gospel lesson today, Jesus tells us that since we love Him, we will each "take up [our] cross" and follow Him. That's a hard idea to understand, so let me explain it to you.

When it was time for Jesus to die for us, soldiers gave Him a great big cross to carry. *If there is a large cross on display, point it out to the children.* That big cross was as big as (bigger than) the cross that's hanging on the wall in our church. That's big, isn't it?

The cross was so big that Jesus probably couldn't pick up the whole cross at once. Instead, He had to drag it on the ground behind Him. He had to pull very hard to move it along the ground. Can you think about dragging a big, heavy cross behind you? How would it feel? You're right. It would be heavy and very hard to do.

The soldiers wanted Jesus to carry the cross all the way to the hill outside of the city. The cross was so heavy that another man had to help Jesus carry it part of the way.

In the Gospel lesson today, Jesus says that if we really love Him, we will be willing to carry our cross and follow Him too. Do you think He was talking about a real cross? Actually Jesus was using the word *cross* as a way of talking about anything that is hard to do. That could be lots of things. Can you think of things Jesus wants us to do that are hard to do? *Allow the children to answer. Respond to their ideas.*

That's right. Doing what our mom and dad want us to do is sometimes hard. Being nice to somebody who is mean to us is very hard to do. Getting ready for bed the first time Mom says to do it is hard too. Smiling and being nice to people even when we don't feel well is another thing that is hard to do. And many times we will have problems—sickness or Mom or Dad losing a job—that feel heavy, like carrying a cross.

Jesus promises to help us when we must deal with these hard things. Let's pray right now for Jesus to help us. *Lead the children in the prayer on the next page or use your own prayer. You may use the prayer as an echo prayer.*

I think you might be able to guess the words to listen for today. That's right. The words today are *Jesus* and *cross*.

As you go back to your seats, I have a small cross to help you remember how much Jesus loves you and how you carry a cross for Him. When you get home today, use your cross to tell about Jesus' love. If you would like two crosses, you could give one to your friend after you finish telling the story. Remember that Jesus loves you so much that He carried that big, heavy cross and then died on it to take away your sins. Isn't that great?

Prayer: Dear Jesus, thank You for loving us so much that You died on the cross to take away our sins. Thank You for forgiving us. Help us do all the things You want us to do. Help us show You just how much we love You. Help us carry our cross, depending on You for help. In Your name we pray. Amen.

Prayer Changes Things

⟹◦⬥◦⟸

SIXTEENTH SUNDAY AFTER PENTECOST: Matt. 18:15–20

Text: "I tell you that if two of you on earth agree about anything you ask for, it will be done for you by My Father in heaven. For where two or three come together in My name, there am I with them." *Matt. 18:19–20*

Teaching aid: Picture or sculpture of praying hands; bookmark that reads "Prayer changes things" or bookmark with a picture of praying hands. A bookmark for each child.

Gospel truth: Jesus listens to us and answers our prayers because He loves us. He is with us always.

Do you think Jesus is here with us right now? Can we see Him? How do you know He's still here? *Allow the children to answer each question.* Sometimes we call this "God's house" because it is a special place where we come to talk to God and learn about Him.

Do you think that God is in other places too? Is He at your house? Is He at school? Is He with you when you play? In the Gospel lesson today, Jesus tells us that whenever there are two or three people together who love Him, He is right there in the middle with them. Isn't that great?

Show the picture or sculpture of praying hands. Who can tell me what these are? *Allow the children to respond.* That's right. These are called praying hands. How do you know they are praying? *Allow the children to answer.* Yes, they are folded and pointing up to heaven.

Some of us pray with our hands together the way they are on the picture (sculpture). Some of us lock our fingers together like this. *Demonstrate each method of folding hands.* Show me how you put your hands when you pray. *Allow the children to demonstrate.* Good, I like the way your hands are folded. We fold our hands to help us remember that we are doing something special. We are talking to God!

God always answers our prayers and does what is best for us. That tells me that God uses prayer to change things. In fact, there is a saying like that: Prayer changes things. I'd like you to say that with me. Prayer changes things. Maybe the grown-ups could say it with us too. *Direct the congregation to say the phrase with the children.*

Jesus tells us that He is with us when we pray and that He is everywhere, not just when we come to church.

Let's pray to Jesus now. I'd like you to help me by saying "Yea, God!" whenever I say, "We just want to say." Let's practice it before we start to pray. *Practice the response. Use the prayer below or a similar one of your own. Emphasize the cue for the children's response of "Yea, God!"*

In church today, listen for the words *prayer* and *Jesus.* Count how many times you hear them.

Can you guess what I have for each of you today? I bought (made) some bookmarks to help you remember how important prayer is. Each of them has a picture of praying hands (or the phrase "Prayer changes things") to help you remember that prayer really does change things. Be sure to tell a friend and a grown-up friend about Jesus this week. Think about who it is you want to tell. Pray to God that He will help you tell your friend the story of His love. Have a great week!

Prayer: Dear God, You are so great that we just want to say (*Yea, God!*). We love You very much. We are happy that You are with us all the time, wherever we are. It makes us want to say (*Yea, God!*). We are happy that You hear our prayers and answer them. In fact, we just want to say (*Yea, God!*). In fact, we want to say again (*Yea, God!*). In Jesus' name we pray. Amen.

God Forgives Me!

———≫◦◦◦≪———

SEVENTEENTH SUNDAY AFTER PENTECOST: Matt. 18:21–35

Text: Then Peter came to Jesus and asked, "Lord, how many times shall I forgive my brother when he sins against me? Up to seven times?" Jesus answered, "I tell you, not seven times, but seventy-seven times." *Matt. 18:21–22*

Teaching aid: Three signs made from poster board that read: "God forgives"; "I'm sorry"; "I forgive you." Make each child a small flag (a pennant made from construction paper taped to a straw) that reads, "God forgives me!"

Gospel truth: God forgives us and helps us forgive one another.

How many of you have ever done anything bad? Could you ever do anything so bad that God might not forgive you or love you anymore? *Allow the children to respond.*

I have good news for you. God always forgives us! He doesn't count how many times we sin or how much we sin. He always forgives us and loves us. *Hold up the first poster (God forgives).* I brought a sign with me that says, "God forgives."

Today's Gospel lesson talks about counting. Peter asked Jesus how many times he needed to forgive someone who did something bad to him. How many times do you think Peter said? *Allow the children to guess.* Those are all good guesses. Peter's idea was that seven was a very big number. Let's all count to seven. *Help the children count.*

If somebody pushed you down *seven* times, that would be a lot of times to forgive that person for pushing you, wouldn't it? But if somebody—let's call him Oscar—kept on pushing you 9, 10, 11, 12 times, what would you do? Would you keep on forgiving Oscar? Would that be easy or hard to do? *Allow the children to respond.* What if Oscar didn't even say this? *Hold up the "I'm sorry" sign.*

What do you think Jesus would say to you about Oscar? What do you think He said to Peter? Remember, Peter thought that forgiving someone seven times would be enough.

Now let's find out what Jesus said. In the Bible, it says that Jesus told Peter that he needed to forgive Oscar 77 times! Wow! Would you really like to forgive Oscar 77 times for punching you or pushing you down? Would it be easy or hard to say this to Oscar? *Hold up the "I forgive you" sign.*

Do you think Jesus stops forgiving us after seven sins? No, He doesn't. Jesus doesn't even count how many times He forgives us. He just keeps on doing it. *Hold up the "God forgives" sign again.* Remember what this says? It says "God forgives."

What Jesus is really telling Peter is that we shouldn't count how many times we forgive Oscar or anybody. We should just keep on loving them and forgiving them, just as Jesus does for us.

Let's say a prayer to Jesus and ask Him to help us. *Lead the children in the prayer below or use your own prayer. Ask the children to echo each phrase.*

I know that Jesus will help you love and forgive your friends each day. There are three words I would like you to listen for today. These words are *forgive* and *sins* and *Jesus.* Can you remember that? Let's say them together to help you remember—*Forgive. Sins. Jesus.*

Today I brought you a flag to help you remember that God forgives you all the time. This flag has words on it. It says "God forgives me!" Let's all say that together. When you show your flag to somebody later today, be sure to tell that person what it says.

Prayer: Dear Jesus, thank You for loving me and forgiving me. Thank You for never counting how many times I do bad things. Help me forgive my friends when they do bad things to me. In Your name I pray. Amen.

The Gift of Heaven

—⟫◆⟪—

EIGHTEENTH SUNDAY AFTER PENTECOST: Matt. 20:1–16

Text: "So the last will be first, and the first will be last." *Matt. 20:16*

Teaching aid: Large gold or copper circle decorated to look like a penny or several large coins such as quarters or fifty-cent pieces; a penny for each child.

Gospel truth: God welcomes into His kingdom everyone who believes in Jesus as Savior. He forgives the sins of each of us, no matter how young or old we are when the Holy Spirit brings us to faith.

How many of you have jobs to do? Do you get paid for those jobs? *Allow the children to answer.* Do you think your mom and dad get paid for their jobs? What if they worked all day and didn't get paid for working? Do you think they would be very happy?

You're right. They would not be very happy. In fact, they would be upset if their boss said, "I changed my mind. I'm not going to pay you for your work."

In the Gospel lesson today, a boss asked lots of people to work for him. He told those that started early in the morning that they would get their pay for the day's work at the end of the day. Some people started later in the morning. The boss told those people that they would get paid at the end of the day, too, but he did not tell them how much that would be.

At lunchtime, the boss found still more people and hired

them too. When it was almost time for people to stop working for the day, he found even more people and put them to work. When it was time to stop working, everybody got in line to get paid. *Hold up the large replica of a coin or several large coins.*

Those workers who had worked the shortest time got paid first. Everybody was surprised when they got paid for a full day's work! "Oh boy," thought those who had worked all day. "If they got paid all that money for just a little work, we're going to get a lot of money today!" Then those who started at lunchtime got paid. They got the same amount. Next those who started during the morning got paid the same amount.

The people who started working early in the morning probably still thought they would get paid more money because they had worked the longest. But do you know what happened? When they got paid, they got the same amount as everyone else! They began to grumble. They went back to the boss and told him they were angry.

What do you think the boss said? He reminded them that they had gotten just what they agreed to work for—a full-day's pay. Do you think the boss cheated them? Not really, did he?

When Jesus got done telling this story, He explained that this was really a story about the kingdom of heaven. If we believe in Jesus, we are like the workers in the story. But it doesn't matter how old or young we are when God's Holy Spirit gives us faith—we will get to heaven just the same because Jesus died for our sins.

This story reminds us that it is important to tell grown-ups, as well as children, about Jesus so they can believe in Him too. Let's thank Jesus today for giving us faith. *Lead the children in the prayer below or use a prayer of your own.*

In church today, listen for the words *faith* and *Jesus.* Maybe you can ask a grown-up to write them down for you so you can look at the words while you are listening to the sermon. Let's say the words together—*Faith. Jesus.*

As you go back to your seats, I have a penny for you. It will help you remember the story of the boss and all the people who worked for him. Remember that Jesus used this story to tell His friends about heaven. He told them that it doesn't matter how old you are when you first believe in Jesus. Use the penny to help you tell a friend about faith in Jesus today.

Prayer: Dear Jesus, thank You for changing our hearts to believe in You. Help us tell others about You so that they can go to heaven. Help us tell children *and* grown-ups just how much You love them. In Your name we pray. Amen.

It's the Heart That Counts

———⟫◆⟪———

NINETEENTH SUNDAY AFTER PENTECOST: Matt. 21:28–32

Text: "Which of the two did what his father wanted?" "The first," they answered. *Matt. 21:31*

Teaching aid: Large, red poster-board heart and large, red poster-board lips; two hand puppets: one to represent the son who obeyed, one to represent the son who did not obey. Also have a small poster-board heart for each child.

Gospel truth: God looks at our hearts and forgives our sins.

Today I'm going to tell you a story about two boys. I want you to listen carefully to figure out which one did what his father wanted him to do. Are you ready?

The father in the story had a big job for his sons to do. He asked them to pick up the toys in their room. Let's give these two boys names. Let's call one Joe and one Mike. *Place the puppets on your hands and identify which is Joe and which is Mike.*

First the father asked Joe to pick up the toys in the room. Now that was a really big job, because Joe and Mike had made a big mess that day. Do you know what Joe said? *Hold up Joe and move him as Joe talks.* He said, "No! I won't! I don't want to!" And off he went to play. *Make Joe walk away and place him to the side.*

Then Dad called for Mike. "Come here," he said. "I have something I want you to do." *Hold up Mike and move him as Mike talks.* "Okay, Dad," said Mike, and he came to see what his father wanted. "I need you to pick up the toys in your room. I want you to clean up the mess right away," said Dad.

"Okay, Dad," said Mike, but he didn't go to his room to start cleaning up. He went outside to play. *Make Mike walk away and place him to the side away from Joe.*

By this time, Joe was feeling really bad. *Pick up Joe.* He thought about what Dad had asked him to do, and he felt sorry for saying no. He went inside and started cleaning the bedroom.

Pick up Mike. Meanwhile Mike kept right on playing. I fooled Dad, he thought to himself. He thinks I'm cleaning up, but it's more fun to play outside.

Let's talk about this story. Which of these two boys did what his father wanted? Was it Joe (*hold up Joe*), who said, "No, I won't," but then changed his mind? Was it Mike (*hold up Mike*), who said, "Yes, I will," but went right outside and started to play instead?

You're right. It was Joe who really did what his dad wanted. What mattered was what happened in his heart (*hold up the poster-board heart*), not what he said with his mouth (*hold up the poster-board lips*). It didn't make his father happy that Joe said no first, but it made him very happy when Joe was sorry and did the job later.

Sometimes we are tempted to say "I don't want to" when we learn what God wants us to do. Then God helps us repent—change our hearts and say we are sorry.

Let's talk to God right now and ask Him to help us be like Joe and do what He asks us to do. *Use the prayer below or your own prayer. You may wish to use an echo prayer.*

Today in church listen for the words *repent* and *Jesus.* Repent is what Joe did when he was sorry for what he had said. Jesus helped change his heart and do what his dad wanted.

As you go back to your seats, I have a special little heart for you to help you remember that Joe's heart was changed to do what his dad asked him to do. When you tell the story to a friend today, you can tell your friend that it's the heart that counts!

Prayer: Dear Jesus, thank You for loving me, even when I do things You don't like. Help me listen to Your Word and do the things that make You happy. Thank You for loving me and forgiving me. Help me always have a willing heart to serve You. In Your name I pray. Amen.

Jesus *Is Coming!*

⇒◆⇐

THIRD-LAST SUNDAY IN THE CHURCH YEAR: Matt. 24:15–28

Text: "For as lightning that comes from the east is visible even in the west, so will be the coming of the Son of Man." *Matt. 24:27*

Teaching aid: Field glasses or binoculars. Make a "looker" (cut out a figure-8 from poster board) for each child. *Optional:* Make binoculars for each child by gluing two pieces of cardboard tubing side by side.

Gospel truth: Jesus will come again to take us to heaven to live with Him forever.

Show the field glasses or binoculars. Have you ever seen some of these before? What do you think I could use these for? *Allow the children to answer.* These are called *binoculars.* I use them when I want to see a long way away.

In the Gospel lesson today, Jesus tells us that He is coming again to take us to heaven to be with Him. Won't that be great? We don't know when that will be, but the Bible tells us that when it happens, we will all know that it is happening.

We won't even need my binoculars. We'll be able to see Jesus just with our eyes. The Bible says that we'll be able to see Jesus from a long way away, just like we can see lightning in the sky from a long way away.

Today I brought a pair of lookers for each of you. I'm going to give them to you now so that we can all "look" for

Jesus together. *Distribute the lookers (or cardboard-tube binoculars).* Look up at the church ceiling. Can you see it any better with your lookers? *Allow the children to answer.*

Can you see Jesus up there? Can you see Jesus on the altar? Let's look at the pews where the grown-ups are sitting. Can you see Jesus sitting there? How about by the door coming into the church? Do you see Jesus there? *Allow the children to respond to each question.*

We can't see Jesus for real anywhere this morning, can we? But we know that He's here. Jesus promises to be with us all the time.

When Jesus comes to take us to heaven, things will be different. Then we will see Him with our eyes. We won't need our lookers. We won't need binoculars. Our eyes will see Him all by themselves.

Let's thank Jesus for loving us and promising to take us to heaven to be with Him. *Use the prayer below or a prayer of your own.*

Listen for two words in church today—*coming* and *Jesus.* When you go home today, be sure to tell a friend about Jesus and how we will see Him when He comes to take us to heaven. Ask your friend if he or she loves Jesus too.

Prayer: Dear Jesus, thank You for loving us so much. Thank You for promising to take us to heaven to be with You. We are excited that we will be able to see You when You come. Thank You for taking away our sins. We love You. In Your name we pray. Amen.

You Did It for Me!

SECOND-LAST SUNDAY IN THE CHURCH YEAR: Matt. 25:31–46

Text: "The King will reply, 'I tell you the truth, whatever you did for one of the least of these brothers of mine, you did it for Me.' " *Matt. 25:40*

Teaching aid: Several pieces of clothing; large drinking cup; sandwich; small paper cup for each child.

Gospel truth: When we do loving things for others, we are doing them for Jesus Himself.

In the Gospel lesson today, we are talking again about the special time when Jesus comes to take us to heaven. Jesus says that He will thank us because when He was hungry we fed Him. *Hold up the sandwich.* What do you think? Did you ever give Jesus a sandwich? Or did you ever give Him clothes to wear? *Hold up the clothing.* Jesus says you did. Or did you ever give Jesus water to drink? *Hold up large drinking cup.* Jesus says you did!

Jesus says that whenever we give food or clothes or even a glass of water to a stranger who needs it, we are giving it to Him. Wow! That's pretty great, isn't it?

(In the following material substitute details of the actual activities in which your church participates.)

That means that when we buy an angel-tree gift or bring food for the food pantry or bring clothes for people who don't have enough to wear, we are buying and bringing those things for Jesus Himself. You might want to talk to your mom or dad about bringing groceries for our Thanksgiving food drive. Those groceries will be given to families who don't have enough to eat.

Also, in a couple of weeks there will be a tree in the back of the church with names of boys and girls on it. Those boys and girls don't have anyone to buy presents for them for Christmas. Your family will be able to choose the name of a boy or girl and buy a present for that person.

Or maybe your family has clothes and blankets that they are not using. You can bring those things to church to our clothing closet. Then people from the church will take those things to people who need them so that they will be able to keep warm this winter.

For most of the things we have been talking about, you need to ask Mom or Dad to help you buy or give things. But Jesus tells us about one more thing He'll thank us for. He says that if you give just a cup of water to someone who is thirsty, you give that water to Jesus too.

Why do we do these nice things, boys and girls? *Allow the children to answer.* We do them because we love Jesus. And we love Jesus because He loved us first and died to take away our sins. That's why He will take us to heaven one day. Then He will say thank you for the good food and the warm clothes and the drink of water you gave Him through others.

Let's ask Jesus to help us share His love with others. *Lead the children in the prayer below or your own prayer.*

There are three words to listen for in church today. Put up three fingers and put one of the words on each finger to help you remember. Here they are: *Jesus* and *give* and *heaven.* Let's say them together to help you remember—*Jesus. Give. Heaven.*

Now I have a small cup to give to each of you. That will help you remember that when we give even a glass of water to someone who needs it, we are helping Jesus. When you tell a friend the story later today, maybe you can each have a glass of water to go along with your story.

Prayer: Dear Jesus, thank You for being so good to us. Thank You for loving us and for dying on the cross to take away our sins. Help us share our love with others in all that we do. In Your name we pray. Amen.

We're Ready!

LAST SUNDAY IN THE CHURCH YEAR:
Matt. 25:1–13

Text: "Therefore keep watch, because you do not know the day or the hour." *Matt. 25:13*

Teaching aid: Outdoor (patio) torch or kerosene lamp—use one that requires kerosene or another fluid as its fuel; small unlit candle for each child.

Gospel truth: Jesus is coming again to take us to be with Him in heaven. Though we don't know when He will come, the faith He strengthens in us makes us ready.

How many of you know what this is? *Hold up the lantern or torch.* In the Gospel lesson today, Jesus tells a story that involves a torch or lantern. It was a light that was used to light the way for a bridegroom to get to the wedding to meet his bride.

In this story, 10 young women were carrying torches. But only five of them brought extra oil to put in their torches after they burned down. The other five did not bring any extra oil.

What do you think happened? At midnight, as the bridegroom was coming, the five who didn't bring extra oil didn't have enough to keep their torches lit. They had to hurry and buy some. They weren't very wise, were they? In fact, Jesus says that they were foolish.

While they were buying oil, the bridegroom came. The five women who had brought extra oil held their torches high so the bridegroom could see the way. *Hold the torch high.* They followed the groom to where the wedding party would be, and they went to the party with everybody else.

After the doors were closed and there was no more room, the other five women came back. What do you think they found? They found a locked door and no way to get into the party.

In this story, Jesus is telling us to be ready because we don't know when He is coming to take us to heaven. We can't say, "Oh, He's not coming yet. I don't have to be ready." That's how the five foolish women thought. They weren't ready when the bridegroom came. But the five wise women were ready, weren't they? And because they were ready, they went to the party—which stands for heaven—with Jesus.

Do you think Jesus wants us to have torches to be ready for heaven? *Allow the children to answer.* No, that's not what He wants. All we need to get to heaven is faith that Jesus died for us and rose again. We are ready for Jesus to come for us right now or anytime because He gives us that faith and keeps us ready. Let's talk to Jesus together. You listen while I say the words. *Use the prayer below or one of your own.*

In church today, listen for three words: *coming* and *ready* and *Jesus*. Let's say those words together—*Coming. Ready. Jesus.*

Today I have a candle for each of you to help you remember the story Jesus told about being ready when He comes. Your candle isn't quite like my torch, but it is still a light to light the way in the dark. When it gets dark later today, ask a grown-up to light your candle for you. Then tell the story again about the five wise and five foolish women in today's story.

Prayer: Dear Jesus, thank You for keeping us ready for heaven. Thank You for loving us and dying on the cross to take away our sins. Thank You for giving us faith through our Baptism and for helping that faith grow. In Your name we pray. Amen.

GRANDPA RULES

GRANDPA RULES

*Notes on Grandfatherhood,
the World's Best Job*

Michael Milligan

Foreword by Bill Cosby

Illustrations by Renee Reeser Zelnick

Skyhorse Publishing

Skyhorse Publishing books may be purchased in bulk at special discounts for sales promotion, corporate gifts, fund raising, or educational purposes. Special editions can also be created to specifications. For details, contact Special Sales Department, Skyhorse Publishing, 307 West 36th Street, 11th Floor, New York, NY 10018 or info@skyhorsepublishing.com.

www.skyhorsepublishing.com

10 9 8 7 6 5 4 3 2 1

Paperback ISBN: 978-1-62914-182-4

Library of Congress Cataloging-in-Publication Data
Milligan, Michael, 1947–
    Grandpa rules : notes on grandfatherhood, the world's greatest job /
Michael Milligan.
        p. cm.
    ISBN 978-1-60239-276-2 (alk. paper)
    1. Grandfathers. 2. Milligan, Michael, 1947– I. Title.
HQ759.9.M55 2008
306.874'5—dc22   2008001480

Printed in China

To Jill, my spectacular and exquisite inspiration.
For everything. And so much more.

CONTENTS

FOREWORD

Before you dig into Mike Milligan's delightfully enter-taining book, *Grandpa Rules*, there are a few things you should know. First, Mike is a very funny writer. Second, his loving and unique take on the wonderful world of grandfather-hood will bring smiles—and, at times, outright laughter—to grandfathers of all ages. And third, Mike promised that if I wrote something nice, he would stop pestering me.

As a proud and loving grandfather myself, I am learning that when my grandchildren visit, I immediately become their oldest stuffed bear and lumpiest trampoline. And as my grandchildren grow, I'll have Mike's book to tell me what to expect next.

So, fellow grandpas, try to remember where you left your pair of 99 Cent Store eyeglasses, grab that pint of ice cream you stashed in the basement freezer for whenever your wife or internist are not around, and sit down and enjoy *Grandpa Rules*.

Happy grandfathering, and remember to deposit the empty ice cream carton in the trash can outside. And do not put the spoon in the dishwasher. Wives notice things like that.

—**Bill Cosby**
August 2007

PREFACE

As I prepared for parenthood many years ago, I was lean, I was clean, and I could remember why I walked from one room into another. And when I became a father for the first time, I had all sorts of guidance to help me in my new role of parenting. First, I could take important life lessons from my father and pass them on to my own children—mysterious pearls from his generation like "Avoid any job where you have to wear a name tag" and "Never drive behind a man with a hat on!"

Or, if I needed guidance that was actually understandable and remotely useful, there were thousands of books offering parenting advice. And if I chose to ignore that advice, I could still use those books to smack my little devils upside the head every so often to get their attention.

But when I learned I would soon be a grandfather, I was surprised to find that there were absolutely no books to help me through this new phase of my life. Oh, sure, there were shelves of books dedicated to grand*mothers*—all with cuddly covers depicting colorful spring bouquets or gentle little lambs.

But there was not a single book jacket that featured a sixty-four-year-old grandfather—napping in a Barcalounger with a cup holder big enough to accommodate a martini shaker—wearing an AC/DC T-shirt that stopped covering his stomach about twelve years earlier.

Then it struck me that there must be countless other grandfathers out there who were experiencing this same feeling of neglect.

Consider this: According to the U.S. Census of 1980—a year when I was in my prime as a father—the population of the United States was 240,132,887.

Today it is 296,496,649, an increase of over 56 million people. This only proves what many of us already know: That we are living longer—no matter what our children have done to shave years off our lives.

It also means that a lot of us are grandfathers, or about to become one.

Another telling statistic is that the United States' current adult population is approximately fifty-one percent female, which suggests that women outlive men. There are probably many scientific explanations for this, but I suspect that somehow a wife adds a few weeks to her life every time she says to her husband, "Don't you think it's time you bought some new undershorts?"

After studying this data, I set out to determine exactly how many grandfathers there are in the United States today. Using my extensive math and statistical talents, and after painstakingly checking and double-checking all my calculations, I can confidently estimate that there are somewhere between 1,827 and 28,382,036 ($\pm3\%$) of us. I realize this number is a bit broad; I could have been much more precise if my computer were working properly. But my grandchildren visited this past weekend and used the keyboard to "play office," and now my desktop is covered with peanut butter and jelly, and my computer will only communicate in Cantonese.

So welcome to my world. In my happy career as a grandfather, I've discovered some universal truths that apply to grandfathers everywhere, and I consider it my pleasure to pass them on to you. For example, I've learned to take it in stride should I hear one of my grandchildren say, "Grandpa sure dresses funny." That's certainly a whole lot better than the child saying, "*Grandma* sure dresses funny; you should have seen what she wore to Grandpa's funeral."

So whether you're a fellow grandpa or a grandfather-in-waiting, I hope this book will guide you as you travel down the road of grandfatherhood.

Because, to borrow a phrase from back in the day ... it's a real trip.

ONE

A GRANDPA? ME?

Yes, you. Because if you're reading this, odds are that you're already a grandfather. Or shuffling your way toward becoming one.

It's also likely that you're a member of the wonderful American generation whose mantra was "Think Young!" Well forty years later, we can *think* whatever we want, but the truth is that we've got more hard miles on us than a '64 Corvair.

And we're leaking oil just as fast.

Where did the years go? What happened to the age of "Sex, Drugs, and Rock and Roll"?

I think I know. We spent a lot of time raising our children and warning them not to do what we did—most of which we never came close to doing. Because if we had, we'd likely be deceased, incarcerated, or living on a Maui mountaintop with my high school friend, Boomer, as he awaits the return of the Lizard King.

And while we were busy with parenting and work, somehow our lives went from Howdy Doody to jury duty.

From McCarthy hearings to hard-of-hearing.

From hi-fi to Wi-Fi.

And though it may hit you like an Ali forearm shiver, it's time to accept that you're actually old enough to be someone's *grandfather*. But how can that be? You dreamed of staying young forever!

Sadly, all of our dreams do not come true. If they did, there would be no more death. There would be no more hunger. There would be no more Michael Bolton albums.

Since becoming a grandfather, I've found it to be unbelievably fulfilling. But I never thought I'd actually *look* like a grandfather. And the first time I had to face that, it was about as fulfilling as a "very special episode" of *My Mother the Car*.

It happened while my wife, Jill, and I were visiting our grandchildren out of town and attending our five-year-old granddaughter's soccer game. Now I don't know about you, but when I was growing up in the fifties and sixties, soccer was not the hugely popular sport it is today, even in Los Angeles. And it certainly wasn't played on manicured suburban fields by perfectly-uniformed, cute granddaughters named Samantha. Rather, it was played on rough-hewn, bottle-strewn lots by prematurely mature fifteen-year-olds with names like Rico and Alfredo who sported moustaches, sleeveless T-shirts, and exotic-looking girlfriends—all of whom were certainly more physically blessed than any of the girls in my tenth grade class.

Except for maybe Joanie Beroni, who had already flunked two grades and who, in three years, would be skating with roller derby's New Jersey Devils.

But back to my granddaughter's game. As I stood on the sidelines with parents of her teammates, a pleasant, outgoing young mother of one of the girls approached and introduced herself.

"Hi," she said perkily. "I'm Christmas's mom."

"*Christmas*," I said, trying to hide my amusement. "What a nice name."

"Yes!" she chirped. "We named her after the most wonderful day of the year."

If I had done that, my oldest son's name would be *July Twelfth*, which—at the age of thirty-one—was the date he finally moved out of the house and into his own apartment.

"Nice to meet you," I said. "I'm Samantha's grandfather."

Like any deluded fifty-five-year-old man who looks in the mirror and sees a thirty-five-year-old stud, I anticipated what would happen next. When Mrs. Christmas heard that I was a grandfather, she would quite likely faint. When she came to, her eyes would grow wide with admiration as she checked out my perfectly understated hoop earring and my slightly graying—yet stylishly shaggy—hair.

"Her *grandfather*?" she'd say. "You're kidding! You don't look old enough to be Sami's grandfather. Her older brother, sure. Or maybe even an uncle. But grandfather? No way!"

"So totally way!" I'd respond, proving that I was as youthful as I looked.

So imagine my shock when Mrs. Christmas didn't come close to fainting … or tweak my earring … or even blink an eye. Instead, she turned to her husband, who was sitting nearby, eating a veggie wrap. "Adam," she barked, "this is Sami's grandfather. Get up and give him your chair. He won't be able to stand for the whole game."

And that was that.

To this suddenly irritating young woman, it was crystal clear that I was old enough to be someone's grandfather.

Later, when I learned that this incredibly insensitive soccer mom was thirty, I wanted to run up to her and say, "Thirty? Let me tell you something, Mrs. Christmas lady: You look at least thirty-two … and a *hard* thirty-two at that! I got ten bucks that says by the time you're fifty, you'll be sagging so badly that you'll try to sue the city for building the sidewalk too close to your breasts!"

All in all, I think I took it pretty well.

★   ★   ★   ★   ★

I tossed and turned in bed that night, and Jill sensed something was not right. "What's bothering you?" she asked.

I sighed. "I can't sleep," I said.

"I knew it," she said. "You snuck those last two taquitos, didn't you?"

"Well, yeah, but…"

"Great," she snapped, getting out of bed and opening all the windows.

After she kissed my forehead and dozed off, I thought back to my own grandfather, a loveable old man who wore a little hat with a feather and plaid Bermuda shorts with calf-high dark socks. A man who said things like "Judas Priest!" "Holy Moses!" and "Yessiree, Bob."

Could I have come to that?

When I finally found sleep, I had a very weird dream. It was 1958 and I was eleven years old. I was rotary-dialing my grandparents' phone number. But I soon realized that in my dream, my grandfather of 1958 had become a "Think Young" grandpa of 2008.

"Hi, Grandma. Is Grandpa home?" I asked when my grandmother answered the phone.

"No, honey, he's working out."

"Oh, in the garage?" I asked. After he retired, my grandfather had turned his garage into a woodworking shop with a lathe, power saws, and other sharp tools. As a result, Grandpa had a living room full of beautiful custom-made wooden furniture, a den with impressive mahogany shelves, and two fingers lopped off at the first knuckle.

Then, in my dream, my grandmother said something very strange.

"No, sweetie. Grandpa's not working out in the garage. He's at the gym."

"The *what*?" I asked.

"The gym. He's working out at the gym."

I couldn't believe what I was hearing. Back in 1958, there weren't gyms on every corner like today. There were only one or two per city, usually located in gritty sections of downtown and sandwiched between a transmission shop and the local bail bondsman. And in those days, there were only two types of people who went into these gyms: boxers whose ears had been slapped into the size of cantaloupes, and tanned and oiled bodybuilders—"weirdos in Speedos," my father called them.

Could it be that my grandfather, sixty-three years old and a lifetime smoker, was about to take up a career in the ring? If so, would he wear plaid Bermuda boxing shorts? And how would they tape his hands with his missing fingertips?

"The gym?" I repeated numbly to my grandmother in my dream.

"Yes," she said with a laugh. "Your grandpa wants to tone up his abs."

Abs? My seven-year-old dream mind wondered if that was what old people called the skin that dangled from their upper arms. Is that where old people kept their muscles?

"When will he be back?" I asked. This was an important phone call; I'd told my dad I needed a new transistor radio to listen to the World Series at school, and he asked me if I thought money grew on trees. What a dumb question, I thought; of course money doesn't grow on trees. It grows in Grandpa's wallet.

"He won't be home for a while," my grandmother said. "After the gym, he's stopping at the spa for a facial, mani-cure, and pedicure."

What?! I didn't know what those first two words were, but a *pedicure*?! I was almost positive that's the same word my parents used last week about that odd, fifty-year-old ex-priest who lived with his mother two blocks away, and who always wanted to play tag with the neighborhood kids until the police gave him a nice ankle bracelet to wear.

"I'll have Grandpa call you when he gets home," my grandmother said. "Or would you rather he text message you?"

"Do *what*?"

"Never mind. Now, if there's nothing else, sweetie, I have to go," said granny, as my dream got even weirder. "I'm off to have a boob job. See you at Christmas!"

That image jolted me awake, and it was then that I realized I needed help with this "grandfather thing."

So let this frightening dream be a lesson to you: At your age, never, ever have more than one taquito before bedtime.

TWO

UNPLANNED GRANDPARENTHOOD

Like many parents, the most life-changing decision I ever made was to have children. The *second* most important decision—once I'd had my kids and gotten to know them—was agreeing to keep them. If children are gifts, how come no one would accept mine when I tried to give them away?

But since we bring our children into the world, we are duty-bound to love them and nurture them and hope that they become responsible and caring adults. It's also important that we provide them with an education that will enable them to accomplish great things, like the ability to read "Apartments for Rent" ads in far-away newspapers before they reach Social Security age.

But you'll find that becoming a grandfather is different. It's not something you have a direct hand in, or worry about, or even think about when you wake up in the middle of the night. I know that when *I* wake up in the middle of the night, my only thought is, "Where did I put the bathroom?"

Since I had no say-so about becoming a grandfather, it only makes sense that I didn't get a vote about the things that began happening as our grandchild's arrival date drew nearer. Even though the soon-to-be-parents lived in their own house three hours away, things began changing in *my*

house. These changes will also happen to *your* house, and when they do, remember that although your name appears on the property deed, you will have very little control over them.

First, don't be surprised if, when your daughter reaches her third month of pregnancy, she calls at least three times per hour to give you progress updates. You should also know that your wife will start doing strange things as well. You see, at my house, Jill hates answering the phone. But with a pregnant daughter, she could flatten five of Snoop Dogg's toughest bodyguards to grab the phone by the second ring.

As soon as she'd hear Dee's voice, Jill would gesture to me and point to our extension phone, indicating that I should immediately pick up and listen in so as not to miss a single word of the report. Like most husbands, I am invited to join this sort of phone conversation with my ears only. Should I make the mistake of actually saying anything, I'm met with, "Shhhh, I can't hear!"

"Hi, sweetie," Jill said.

"Hey, Mom. How are you guys doin'?"

"We're fine," Jill claimed, speaking for both of us.

But when Jill said we both were "fine," she was only telling *half* the truth—which is that *she* feels fine because she'd had a nice afternoon nap—while I, a man rapidly nearing grandfather age, am inexplicably forbidden from taking naps, even if I've been forced to listen to John Tesh's music after running a marathon . . . uphill.

In fact, just a few hours before this phone call from Dee, I was sitting in my favorite chair, reading the newspaper and still adjusting to the beautiful silence that moved into the house when the children moved out. And while I was enjoying the sports page, Jill bounded down the stairs, looking refreshed.

"Hello, sweetheart," I said. "How was your nap?"

I've noticed that the word "nap" can change a normally pleasant and lovely wife into something evil. It can cause her neck veins to bulge, her mouth to tighten, and her nose to shoot a stream of hateful fire at you.

"Nap?" Jill hissed as her head made a complete 360. "What makes you think I was taking a nap?!"

I paused. "Well . . ."

She glared.

"I went up to the bedroom to find my glasses . . ."

"And?"

"And I saw you lying on the bed."

"So?"

"So, your eyes were closed, you were making a noise just like the dog makes when he's sleeping, and there was just a little bit of drool coming from the side of your mouth. I put it all together."

Her eyes became scary, bright red circles. If you're a long-time husband, you already know this sign: Your wife is about to say something that should not be forgotten.

"Nice try, Clouseau, but I was *not* taking a nap!" Jill said. "I was resting my eyes."

"Oh," I said, smugly. "Well, what about yesterday when I dozed off and you woke me because I was taking a nap? What's the difference?"

"*What's the difference*?" she sputtered. "*You* were on the sofa in the den. Anyone could just walk right in and see you there with your mouth wide open."

Unless our home had also become our city's bus station, I wondered who would be walking through my den in the middle of the afternoon. It's just the two of us since the children moved away. And it couldn't be one of them, because I changed the security code before they hit the end of the driveway.

Then I recalled an animal program I had seen about lions. Husband lions have the right idea; they just lay around all day while the wife goes out for food. It's good to be King of the Jungle. Not Queen of the Jungle, or Prince of the Jungle. The King—a guy who can go out in public no matter how goofy his hair looks. And what brave deeds must the husband lion perform to warrant being King? Well, every once in a while he must roar to warn beasts—and noisy children—not to fool with him. I imagined how the King would feel if a lioness treated her husband in the same manner as her human counterpart.

The wife lion comes home, dragging dinner behind her, only to find her husband fast asleep in his lion's den.

"Hey, Mr. Big Time King, wake up!" she growls, scratching him and then biting his leg for good measure. "What do you think you're doing?"

"I was, uh, listening to the news coming over the jungle drums," says the husband lion, covering a yawn.

"You were taking a nap!"

"I wasn't taking a nap," he says. "I was resting my eyes."

"No, you were taking a nap!" she insists. "I saw you! And I'll bet everyone else saw you, too!"

"Everyone else? Like who?"

"The hyenas for starters. Hear them laughing? They probably walked by and saw you snoring with your mouth wide open."

"Okay, sweetie," the lion confesses. "Maybe I was having a catnap. Sorry."

"All right," she says, dropping supper at his paws. "But if it happens one more time, you're going out to catch your own wildebeest."

★　★　★　★　★

Back on the telephone, Jill asked, "How are *you* feeling, honey?"

"Amazing," Dee said. "This pregnancy thing soooooo agrees with me. I want to have six or maybe even seven."

As I covered the mouthpiece to hide my laughter, Dee mentioned that she felt the baby kick today. "I think we may have a punter. Or a Rockette," she said.

I thought about that, and since a Rockette has a guaranteed job for only three freezing weeks a year, I hoped for a punter.

The conversation continued for nearly an hour, but I quietly logged off when the ladies started discussing whether the motif of the baby's room should be early Bert and Ernie or retro Winnie the Pooh.

I recall another "update" three months later, when Dee was entering her eighth month of pregnancy. The temperature in her town had been over 100 degrees for so long that she and her husband were considering a move to someplace cooler—a corrugated metal duplex in Death Valley.

When the phone rang, I answered because Jill was out in the garage, antiquing a layette for the baby.

"Oh, hi, Dee," I said. "How are you feeling?"

"Feeling?!" she screamed. Suddenly, Mrs. Loves-to-Have-Babies had turned into Pregzilla. "My back hurts more than a Russian power lifter's. My hair has all the body of a Raggedy Ann doll; my emotions go from happy, to sad, to euphoric, to panic-stricken—all within ten exhilarating minutes! And don't tell me that I have that special glow. If I wanted a glow, I'd go to a tanning booth! I'm bigger than a manatee; I'm retaining more water than the Hoover Dam; and I need a forklift just to get out of the chair! How do you think I'm feeling?!"

Fortunately, my years of parenting had taught me exactly what to do in this situation.

I yelled out to the garage, "Jill, it's for you!"

But what if you're the father of a son who's about to become a father himself? Expect the phone calls to be far less frequent. And more general in nature.

"Hey! Everything all right?" you ask when he calls.

"Yeah."

"And my favorite daughter-in-law is feeling good?"

"Yeah."

"Good."

"Yeah."

Then there's silence. You know that he wants to talk to you about something, but you also know that speech was his least favorite subject in high school.

"Did you call to say something other than *yeah*?"

"Yeah. See, Dad, I went out to one of those furniture warehouses today and bought a crib, but when I got it home, all the assembly instructions were in Swedish. I could use some help putting it together."

"No problem," you say confidently, proud of him for acknowledging he needs help to do the job right.

"Honey, it's for you," you call, holding the phone out for your wife.

That night in bed when I put my arm around Jill, I was hit with a disconcerting thought. "It's gonna be weird," I said. "I've never slept with a grandma before."

"Keep talking like that, old man, and you never will," she said with a laugh. Then she kissed me and drifted off into a grandmother's dreams of bassinets and mobiles.

"Old man, hmm?" I thought. Maybe she's got a point. After all, I wasn't exactly "young." And whether I liked it or not, most people under twenty-five think that anyone who doesn't have an iPhone must've fought alongside Davy Crockett.

But "old man"?

Then, the more I thought about it, I realized this whole thing might have a huge upside.

I mean, what kind of wife would refuse an old man a decent nap?

THREE

THINGS THAT GO BEEP IN THE NIGHT

There was another change in our house that indicated the big day was drawing near: My loving wife, the soon-to-be grandmother who believes that cell phones are technology's way of interrupting valuable family time, began wearing a pager.

She took it with her everywhere, which meant her pager went to much nicer places than I did.

And because it was intended for emergency use only, I, of course, was not allowed to have the number.

"But what if I'm trimming the hedge in the yard and the clippers slip and I cut off both of my legs? Isn't that an emergency?" I asked.

"You doing yard work is not an emergency," she informed me. "It's a miracle."

And then, one night . . . BEEP!

I tried to wake up as quickly as possible. But in the time it took me to pry my eyes open, Jill had somehow managed to shower, dress, and visit her hairdresser.

"Get up!" she said. "It's time!"

"Time for what?" I mumbled, trying to clear the cobwebs.

"The baby's coming!"

"Here?"

"Will you please wake up? The kids are leaving for the hospital."

"Maybe it's false labor," I suggested, hoping for a few more hours of sleep, since I'm not allowed to nap.

"No, it's the real thing. Look."

She showed me her beeper.

"See? *9-9-9!*" she said.

"What does *that* mean?" I asked, fighting to separate my lips and wondering who had put the glue on them while I was sleeping.

"It means," she said matter-of-factly, "that Dee's contractions are thirty minutes apart."

As I stumbled out of bed, I asked why 9-9-9 represents *30* minutes. Why not *30-30-30?*

"It's our special code," she explained in a way that only wives can explain. Simply put, she meant that the code should be obvious to any idiot.

Any idiot, that is, except me.

And as I reached for my most comfortable clothes, I imagined a foreign spy submarine submerged just off the coast of Santa Monica.

"9-9-9," says the head spy. "What do you think that means?"

"It's some kind of complicated code," says the assistant spy. "Darn! I believe those women have outsmarted us again. We'll never find out when that child is going to be born."

"Okay, I'm ready to go," I told her.

As I started out, she looked at my outfit. "You're actually going to wear that old sweat suit?"

I looked at the clock on the nightstand. I was not aware the hospital had a dress code, particularly at 4:30 a.m., which is about when we'd arrive after our 300-mile drive.

"No one's going to see me," I explained.

"Our *grandchild* will. And do you want that to be the first thing she sees you in?"

I explained that I had read somewhere that babies don't have clear vision until they're two or three days old. I suspect that this is nature's way of shielding their new eyes from old people who squint at them while saying things like "wooo-baaa-bee-bee" in a falsetto that only Tiny Tim would appreciate. Because if newborns were forced to see such things, they could grow up to be chain smokers or even waffle iron repairmen. Or both.

And with that, I defiantly strode toward the door, wearing my comfortable old sweat suit. I'm as nice as the next guy, but sometimes a man has to put his foot down, even if it's wearing an old slipper.

When we hurried into the hospital about five hours later, the slacks and shirt that Jill dressed me in still looked fresh, even after the long drive. When I asked an orderly for directions to the maternity ward, he checked my attire and said, "I'll take you there myself, doc."

We arrived as they were wheeling Dee toward the delivery room. She wasn't particularly happy, but seemed to be doing much better than her husband, who looked like a man who had just consumed a gallon of very bad clam dip on a very hot day. Jill ran to Dee's side and kissed her.

"Don't worry, honey. Everything will be fine."

"That's right," I said, patting her hand. "Good luck, love. I'll see you when you're a mom."

"Wait a minute," the father-to-be said to me. "You're not going in to see it?" I immediately recognized this as a case of misery loving company.

"No, Ron, I'm not."

"How come?"

I wanted to tell him that there are two things a man does not want to see: His daughter in pain, and his daughter in stirrups.

Plus, I was dressed too nicely.

But instead, I said "because it's something a husband and wife should share together."

"But *Jill*'s going to be in there," he said as a nurse handed him a gown and mask.

And there it was: my first glimpse into one of the many differences between grandmothers and grandfathers.

When the chips are down, grandmothers can be counted on to do whatever's necessary.

When the chips are down for grandfathers, we just go into the kitchen and get more chips.

I spent the next forty-five minutes pacing and perspiring and wishing I'd worn my old sweat suit. Then Jill came out of the delivery room, and when she removed her mask, I could see her big smile.

She ran into my arms and all she could say through her tears was, "She's beautiful."

A little while later we went in to visit the new mother.

"How do you feel?" I asked Dee.

"Amazing! What an incredible experience!"

Incredible? This young woman had just gone through what is arguably the most painful and grueling of physical demands, and she describes it as "amazing"? Can this be the same person who once forged her mother's signature on a high school P.E. slip to get out of jogging one lap around the track because "she didn't want to smell gnarly"?

Soon a nurse came in with the baby. When Jill had said she was beautiful, I'd smiled politely because all fathers hear that when their own children our born. But in truth, most babies look more like newborn pterodactyls from *Jurassic Park* than human beings.

I've found that babies normally don't become "beautiful" until they're about two weeks old. And they stay beautiful until they're teenagers, when the only thing beautiful about them is that in a few short years you can ship them off to college.

But this child *was* absolutely beautiful. The most gorgeous child I had ever seen! Man, this grandfather thing was coming pretty easy to me.

Our son-in-law grabbed a camera and snapped a picture of me holding my new granddaughter.

Three days later, that picture was proudly posted on our refrigerator, where it has remained for the past thirteen years, and is now surrounded by pictures of our other grandchildren in various stages of growth and toothlessness.

And whenever I look at that particular picture, I'm able to recount every little detail of the day I first became a grandfather. And even after all this time, I still pat myself on the back, because—for such an important occasion—I stood firm and didn't let Jill talk me into wearing that ragged old sweat suit.

FOUR

WHO'S YOUR (GRAND)DADDY?

Unfortunately, U.S. divorce rates have more than doubled since 1950, so it follows that many babies born today will have more than two grandfathers, especially if these babies have grand*mothers* from the sixties who still wear tie-dye and use words like *groovy* and *bitchin'* to describe their latest tattoos.

Although many of my era came into the world with only two sets of grandparents, it's common for today's children to have family trees with the names of more grandfathers than the obituary page of the *Miami Herald*.

Of course, while many of today's new grandfathers will continue to have a direct biological link to their grand-children, this is not an absolute necessity. There are other important qualities that help one qualify. These include:

- a willingness to watch the same singing starfish video so many times that you'd like to donate your corneas *before* you're dead,
- knowing the difference between Hannah Montana and Mona Arizona,
- and developing the ability to sleep in a bed while your three-year-old granddaughter thrashes, twists, turns, and digs her toes into areas of your body that you'd rather she didn't.

And as the rate of multiple marriages continues to increase, I have discovered a new subculture of middle-aged men I call G.B.M.s (Grandfathers by Marriage).

The important thing to remember in all of this is that *grandfather* is more than a title. It's a feeling.

Let's say an older man marries a woman who already has college-age grandchildren. It's not likely that her grandchildren would suddenly begin calling him "Grandpa." Nor, I suspect, would the man truly *feel* like a grandfather to them. It's more likely they would call him "the nice old guy who's sleeping with Grandma." There is a problem with that, though: For his birthday, it would be very hard to find a greeting card with that title on it.

Now I'd like to tell you about my good friend, Pete. His nineteen-year marriage produced one child, a son whom he loved without reservation. But when his marriage ended, so did Pete's self-esteem, and other than visits with his son, he spent the next year living in a drab rental apartment and going out about as often as the Unabomber.

And whenever he needed cheering up, he'd rent a copy of *Kramer vs. Kramer.*

And as much as his friends tried, Pete declined countless invitations for dinner, movies and, of course, blind dates. But finally, Pete agreed to go with us to the wedding of a mutual friend's daughter, but only after receiving a call from the bride-to-be telling him that she couldn't think of a better wedding present than having him there.

Pete is known as a very thrifty man, and I've always wondered if this call got to him on an emotional level, or because it offered him a chance to save a hundred bucks and a trip to the mall where he might run into someone he knew.

In any event, Pete sat with us during the ceremony and only dabbed his eyes once . . . at the "till death do us part" part.

But as it turned out, those were the last tears Pete would shed for quite a while. During the reception, while Pete was alone at the bar sulking and nursing his third Shirley Temple, a woman named Lauren approached and ordered a Nancy Lopez. The bartender was stumped; and when Lauren explained that a Nancy Lopez was an Arnold Palmer with a dash of Tabasco, Pete couldn't help chuckling. That led Lauren to strike up a conversation and before long, the two of them discovered that they had an awful lot in common. Lauren, too, had recently come out of a long-term marriage and also had to be goaded into attending the wedding. They were about the same age. They each had one child—Lauren a daughter who was a year younger than Pete's son. What's more, they learned that they had both attended UCLA and were avid Bruins fans. And if that weren't enough, on the drive home, Pete giddily told us the ultimate coincidence: He *sold* books, and Lauren *read* books!

They began going out regularly, and have been blissfully wed for the past ten years. Lauren's daughter has also since married, and five years ago she called Pete and Lauren to announce that she was pregnant.

They were both thrilled at the news, with Pete being particularly happy for Lauren. He confessed to me that he was also a bit jealous, in that it wasn't his child who was having the baby. I reminded him that his son Jason was happily married and surely Pete would be receiving the same kind of phone call very soon.

(Note: As it turns out, "happily married" and "very soon" proved to be a bit optimistic, because Jason was divorced a short time later. Shattered by the experience, Jason has expressed no desire to re-marry or even seriously date, instead resigning himself, at age thirty-four, to spending the rest of his life living with his mother. This is unacceptable to Pete, who has put himself on Red Alert to find a young lady to help Jason out of his funk. In his sales job, Pete has met several perfect candidates, but Jason has dismissed each of them after only one date. So, recently, Pete has had to relax his standards for a prospective daughter-in-law, and will now consider any young lady so long as she has never worked for either the Mayflower Madam or Heidi Fleiss.)

From the outset of her pregnancy, Lauren's daughter affectionately began calling Pete "Grandpa," even though the baby would have two "real" grandfathers, both of whom were extremely good and decent men. Yet as much as everyone treated him like family, Pete couldn't help feeling like an outsider.

So I told Pete about my Uncle Leo, a really funny guy who was married to my Aunt Marie. Leo was far and away my favorite uncle, partly because whenever the family got together, my other uncles wore slacks and dress shirts, while Uncle Leo sported dark blue jeans and a T-shirt with rolled-up sleeves, which provided him an excellent storage area for his cigarettes.

My other uncles were nice enough, but they were always arguing politics with each other, whereas Uncle Leo preferred talking with me and, more surprisingly, listening to what I had to say. Uncle Leo and Aunt Marie had no children of their own, and I suspected that if Leo ever had a son, he'd want one like me.

Uncle Leo made his living as a handyman, and whenever he told his "fix-it" stories, he'd always let fly with a few "damns" and "sonofabitches." Then he'd wink at me, knowing that such language titillated my young Roman Catholic ears and irritated the hell out my parents, which I assumed was the reason they didn't seem to have the same affection for Uncle Leo that I did. I truly loved Leo, and was saddened when he and Aunt Marie moved to Ohio. I never saw him again, but I thought of him often . . . particularly when I saw a man with hard-pack Marlboros rolled up in his sleeve.

Years later, when I wanted invite Leo and Marie to my wedding, I couldn't understand my mother's resistance. "Of course Marie will come," she told me. "But not that Leo."

That Leo? What happened? Had they divorced? Had Leo died? Or worse, had he become a Democrat?

Finally Mom admitted the truth: Uncle Leo and Aunt Marie were never really married. They'd been "living in sin" all those years . . . until Leo ran off with "some trollop he met at a package store." My mother sighed. "He's not your real uncle, Mike. We just called him that to make him feel like family."

But after I thought about that for a while, I realized that it didn't matter who Leo was or wasn't married to—he was my favorite uncle, and nothing could change that. And I told Pete that if he could be as kind and loving and important to his grandchild as Leo was to me, then he would be a wonderful grandfather.

A *real* one.

Then came the big day: Lauren's granddaughter was born.

She and Pete were there for the birth, and soon went in to see the new mother and baby. That was when Lauren's daughter gently handed Pete the newborn with the instruction "Say hello to your granddaughter."

Pete later told me that when he stared into the baby's amazingly dark eyes, he thought a thousand thoughts about what wonderful things this child would bring to him and Lauren . . . and to all her grandparents. Then Pete realized that he had better hand the baby back to her mother and excuse himself.

He knew he was about to cry and he preferred to do it in private.

As Pete and Lauren's granddaughter has grown, it's obvious that this now rosy-cheeked four-year-old adores Pete. The child has proven over and over again that she loves him as her grandfather; hugs and kisses him as her grandfather; and asks him for money as her grandfather. And Pete knows there's no doubt about it . . . he's her grandfather.

★   ★   ★   ★   ★

A few years ago, Jill and I had just returned from a weekend visiting our grandkids, when my sister called to say that Leo had died.

The next evening, I landed in Cincinnati and made it to the funeral home just in time for Leo's Rosary, held the night before his burial Mass. Many people think that Catholics—particularly Irish ones—spread out the funeral process over two days so that they'll have an excuse to tip a few more.

Well, I can tell you that this is absolutely untrue.

We don't need an excuse.

Out in front after the Rosary, I learned that Leo had married "the trollop," and that they'd had two kids who were now parents themselves. And even in their grief, I could tell that they were a family of great joy.

As I stood there alone, a woman approached and asked me if I was related to Leo. I thought about that for a moment, then said, "I sure am. He was my uncle. My favorite one."

FIVE

THE NAME GAME

At birth, the first thing we're given is a heartbeat. The second thing is a name. Some parents name their children after a family member or a friend. Some parents name their children after historical figures. And it seems that some of today's young parents name their children after too many Jägermeisters.

As the arrival of our grandchild drew near, we received regular calls from the soon-to-be parents, telling us the latest names they were considering for the baby.

"If it's a boy, we're thinking *LaSalle*; if it's a girl, *Nova*."

I wondered if they were giving birth to a child or a sedan. As I was about to suggest that the baby should have a mechanic instead of a pediatrician, Jill's look told me that if I said another word, it would be my final one.

But whatever the parents' selection process, one of the first things a baby learns—right after learning how to make such a big smell come from such a little body—is its name. Our youngest granddaughter is named Claire. She loves me, but if she's playing in her crib and I say, "Hello there, Steve," she will not respond. She may, however, think that I have forgotten to take my ginkgo biloba.

That's why a name is important; you grow up with it, secure that it will always be yours. No one can take it from you. You will have it until you go to your grave. Or until you become a grandfather . . . whichever comes first.

For those of you who are very new grandfathers, it's likely that you've spent more than a few hours thinking about what you'd like your grandchild to call you. Some of you may settle on the ever-popular "Grandpa Handsome." Others may opt for something a bit more subtle, like "Grandpa Favorite."

But before you give it any more thought, you need to pay close attention to what I am about to tell you.

You have no choice in the matter.

The baby will decide what to call you. So get used to the fact that your naming will be left to a creature whose greatest achievement has been sleeping through the night without pooping.

And whatever name your first grandchild gives you—no matter how foolish—it will continue to be your name for every grandchild that follows. When my oldest grandchild, Sydni, was about seven months old, she pointed at up me and gurgled what sounded to everyone like "Buh-Buh!"

"Did you hear that?" her mother cried out.

"She called you Buh-Buh!" her father said, patting me on the back with such excitement that you'd think the child had just recited the Gettysburg Address. In Latin. I, on the other hand, will never know what my beautiful granddaughter was trying to say that day. For all I know, "Buh-Buh" could have been her way of saying, "Hey, if you all think strained carrots are so tasty, why don't *you* eat them?"

But I had no choice in the matter, so for the rest of my life as a grandfather, I will be "Buh-Buh." I've grown to like it; and although it may lack pizzazz, it'd certainly garner me some attention should I ever start hanging with the NASCAR crowd.

But why "Buh-Buh"? What made those sounds come out of her mouth? While pondering this, I realized that an infant's "vocabulary" is limited by the sounds it can make. And this led me to one of my greatest grandfather discoveries to date:

THE BABY ALPHABET

Normally by the age of three or so, a child gains command of all twenty-six letters of the alphabet. Children will use all these letters until the age of thirteen, when they stop using the letter "g" at the end of "ing" words. They will continue this practice until they apply for their first real job, which should ideally occur before they reach the age of thirty-six.

I have observed that for the first year or so of a baby's life, its alphabet seems to consist of only eleven letters: A, B, D, E, I, M, N, O, P, T, and U. To prove this theory, all I had to do was observe Sydni cooing to herself in her crib.

"Tuh-muh-bee-duh-poe-tee-nuh," is what she mumbled as she saw me staring down at her. That can be loosely translated to mean, "When I get as old as that man, will I have hair in *my* nose?"

Vowels are easy for a baby because *a, e, i, o,* and *u* require very little tongue development. And as any parent knows, a child's tongue can only be fully developed by sticking it out at his brothers and sisters.

Some consonants are easy for babies, too. The easiest one for infants—and therefore the most popular—is the letter "M." This is probably why the first "word" many infants utter is "mama." It is also why their second word is usually *money.*

Other consonants, however, are much more difficult for them. Take the letter "K." There's just too much tongue/palate coordination required. So if you're expecting your grandchild to call you by your name and your name is Keokuk, you might want to go on vacation until the child begins shaving. Or get a legal name change.

To prove my point, let me tell you a story about my friend, Craig. Craig is a bear of a man; and I use the term "bear" literally, because several times Craig has broken into my refrigerator and eaten all my food. A former college football linebacker and retired policeman, Craig has spent a lifetime holding his own against the biggest and baddest around. But as a father and grandfather, he is the gentlest, kindest, most nurturing man since Mister Rogers. But Mister Rogers sang better and looked a lot nicer in a cardigan.

Craig visited his new grandson daily. He'd gently hold the infant in his burly arms and say, "Hi, little man. I'm your Grandpa Craig. Can you say *Grandpa Craig*?" Most of the time, the child would stare at him and burp. Other times the baby would suddenly begin kicking his legs and jerking his arms spasmodically, like an overturned turtle. But never, ever did the baby say "Grandpa Craig." Or anything even close to it.

But then one day, there was an apparent breakthrough. After visiting his grandson, Craig came over to our house, thrilled. In fact, he was so excited that he constructed and downed *two* Reuben sandwiches.

"Okay," he said, explaining his joy, "I'm holding the baby like I always do and I say, 'Can you say "Grandpa Craig"?' And you know what he did? He looked right at me and said *mee-dah*!"

Mee-dah?

"And it was clear as a bell, too! Swear to God! The kid's almost got it!"

I looked at Craig and feared that an overdose of sauerkraut and spicy mustard was causing frontal lobe gastritis.

When I told him that I didn't see the connection, Craig was dumbfounded by my lack of vision.

"Don't you see? *'Grandpa Craig? Mee-dah?'* We're definitely on the right track. I'm beginning to think the kid might be a genius."

Maybe so, but the little genius never uttered those two syllables again.

Craig was crestfallen until several weeks later, when he answered the phone at home one evening.

On the line, a strange female voice said, "Tay-Tay?"

Craig wondered what poor fool would have a name like that.

"Tay-Tay? Sorry, but there's no Tay-Tay here," Craig informed the caller.

"Oh, but I think there is," she said.

"No, I'm afraid you have the wrong number. Good night."

But before he could hang up, he heard, "Daddy, it's me!"

Craig realized it was his daughter, who had been speaking in that annoying baby talk we all used when we were new parents.

"He said it, Daddy! The baby said your name!"

Craig was thrilled. "He said 'Grandpa Craig'?"

"No," said his daughter. "*Tay-Tay!* That's what he calls you!"

(Note: I later explained to Grandpa Craig that in the baby alphabet, the difficult consonants "C" and "R" apparently became a "T," the easy "AY" sound stayed "AY," and that the child dropped the "G" at the end. So at least in this respect, his grandson was about twelve years ahead of his time.)

His daughter continued, "I held up your picture and said, 'Who's this, honey?' He looked at it and said, 'Tay-Tay.'"

"Really?" said Craig, on cloud nine.

"Really. And he did it three different times. Isn't that precious?"

And at that moment, it was "Good-bye, Craig; hello, Tay-Tay!"

The very next day, Craig went to the Department of Motor Vehicles to order personalized "TAY-TAY" license plates. Not surprisingly, they were still available.

And a week later, when the four of us went out to dinner, Craig and his wife approached the hostess about their reservation.

"Your name?" the hostess asked.

"Smith," said Craig's wife.

"No, it's under Tay-Tay," Craig said proudly.

Now, do you need you any further proof that becoming a grandfather can lead a grown man to do some wonderfully goofy things?

And it's not just Craig. For centuries, seemingly intelligent men have been putty in their grandchildren's chubby little hands.

There's a story—from Aeschylus I believe, or maybe it was Neil Simon (I always confuse the two)—about two grandfathers in ancient Greece who were known to their grandchildren as PoPo and Dah-Bee. One day, PoPo was out for a walk with his young grandson when he spotted Dah-Bee approaching with his grandchild. PoPo and Dah-Bee were fast friends who often whiled away lazy Athens afternoons debating such weighty topics as the finality of death, the efficacy of democracy, and the origins of the age-old conundrum *I know you are, but what am I?*

This day, the men stopped to talk, but before long their grandkids grew antsy and started giving each other wedgies. Finally, PoPo's grandson said to him, "I'm hungry, PoPo. Can we get stop at McBaklava's on the way home?"

Then the other little one said to his grandfather, "I want to go, too. And don't forget, Dah-Bee, we promised Grandma we'd pick up her toga at the cleaners. She gave you her ticket and told you not to lose it, remember?"

"Of course I remember," said Dah-Bee.

PoPo and Dah-Bee smiled at each other as Dah-Bee said to his friend, "See you tomorrow, Plato."

"You got it, Socrates," PoPo said, taking his grandson's hand and heading off to get something to eat.

After Socrates waved good-bye, he began searching his robes for his wife's laundry ticket. He knew he had it somewhere.

SIX

RIGHT OFF THE SHOWROOM FLOOR

Of course, the biggest difference between having your own children and having grandchildren is one that brings the greatest joy to grandparents: you can love them. You can kiss them. And then, after you've spoiled them, you can send them back to where they came from.

I've found that a helpful way to fully understand the differences between your children and your grandchildren is to compare them to automobiles.

Your own children are like the family car.

Remember when you brought home your first new car? As soon as the neighbors saw you pull into your driveway, they came over to admire it.

"What a beauty," one said.

"Mmm, mmm," said another, taking a deep whiff. "There's nothing like the smell of a new one."

"Seeing yours makes me want to have one, too," said the neighbor who was always trying to keep up with the Joneses, even though the Joneses got divorced and moved far away two years ago.

These are the same things they said when you brought home your first child.

But as your child got older, the neighbors became less enamored with it, and sometimes wished that you'd trade it in for a newer, quieter one. Especially when it got to be about ten years old and started making funny noises that often resulted in unpleasant odors.

Just like your family car.

And several years later, when you brought another new one home, the neighbors hardly seemed to notice. And even though you got a new one, you and your wife decided to keep the older one as well, believing—in spite of all the evidence against it—that someday it might actually become a *classic*. And should that happen, all the time and money you spent on maintenance would be well worth it. As the years passed, whenever you brought home other new ones, you always hung on to your older ones, even though they had become increasingly expensive to maintain.

You provided them with regular check-ups, offered plenty of tender loving care, and tried to keep them clean. Yet no matter what you did, they seemed to drop off in performance the older they got. Eventually, you had to face the harsh reality that none of them was likely to become a classic. But because of their great sentimental value, you couldn't get rid of them. Sure, sometimes they went out for a test drive, but they always seemed to end up back at your house.

Your grandchildren, on the other hand, are fun new rental cars. Normally, you only have them for a few days, and when you first pick them up, they are clean, shiny, and full of gas. You will decline the extra insurance because you're experienced . . . you know what you're doing. You tell the people who own the rental car not to worry . . . you've been doing this since they were born!

But still, they'll give you pages of instructions before they'll let you take the car, and they'll insist on telling you what kind of fuel it takes and how often it takes it. They'll tell you what to do if it has an oil leak. They'll even give you an after-hours number to call in case of emergency.

Then the last thing they'll tell you is not to take the rental car to certain places.

That's when you and your wife smile, because now you know exactly where you're going first.

After all, what's so wrong with the car getting a little mud on it? You'll be returning it Sunday night, and if it's dirty, so what? It's not like they'll never rent you the car again.

So you spend the entire weekend taking the rental car places you haven't been in years.

You go to the beach, and get sand all over it.

You go to the amusement park, and get cotton candy all over it.

You go to the kiddy pizza place with the scary clown and get vomit all over it.

And of course you take it to visit all your friends, so they can see how lucky you are to have such a beautiful new model.

And then, after you and your wife have enjoyed enjoy a fun-filled, wonderful weekend with your beautiful rental, you get to return it. And even though you're both exhausted, your wife will insist on washing it before you drop it off.

And when you do, the rental car will look exactly like it did when you picked it up. You'll tell the rental agents how much you enjoyed every minute of the two days and how good the car was.

And as you go to sleep Sunday night, you try to remember every precious detail of your weekend so you can tell your co-workers all about it as soon as you walk into the office the next morning.

But when you try to get out of bed on Monday, you realize you won't be walking *anywhere* soon, unless your bed grows legs. This is because you've made the mistake that most grandparents make: After a hectic and fun-filled weekend with your rental car, you've fooled yourself into thinking that you can rebound just like you did when you were a teenager. But you are not a teenager. Unless you give your age in German Shepherd years.

Based on my experience, here's what will happen after your wild weekend with your rental car: When you realize your legs feel like wet linguine, you will turn to your wife for help. But she will be lying flat on her back, eyes wide open, blankly staring at the ceiling.

"Darling?" you say.

"Ungh," she mumbles.

"How do you feel?"

"Ungh."

"Is it like you've been hit by a convoy of lumber trucks?"

"Ungh."

"Then I don't suppose you could help me find my feet."

"Ungh."

It will take at least twenty minutes before your legs will start receiving commands from your brain. And when you're finally able to hobble toward the bathroom, you will do it with the help of your late mother-in-law's old walker that was folded under the bed. It's at times like these you're thankful that your wife never throws anything away. And when you look at the legs of the walker, you also solve the mystery of what happened to some of your old tennis balls.

After an hour in the bathroom, you make it to the phone and dial very carefully, because even the ends of your fingers are exhausted. You call your office and tell them you won't be in today.

"What's wrong? You really sound beat."

"Yeah. I think it's the flu or something. I had it all weekend."

"Really? Because Charlie here thought he saw you going into that crazy pizza place with your grandkid on Saturday."

There's only one thing you can say to that.

"Ungh."

"You be in tomorrow?"

"Ungh."

"Good. See you then. And feel better."

"Ungh."

Later that day, when you've made your way to the kitchen, you discover something that probably would have prevented you from getting to work on time, even if you *had* felt better that morning. When you put your dirty cereal bowl in the dishwasher, you spot your wallet on the bottom rack. Apparently your granddaughter decided that was a good place to store it when she was playing "ATM."

And later, you also discover that the bureau containing your undershorts has been mysteriously locked and you can't open it. Because the key, which you hid in a place where no one could possibly find it, is missing.

This teaches you an important grandfather lesson: There is no hiding place that's safe from your grandkids. If we were serious about finding Osama bin Laden, we would just send out a posse of four-year-olds to hunt him down.

When Monday night rolls around, do not be concerned if you go to bed very early and fall asleep before the news.

The six o'clock news.

I've learned that it normally takes about forty-eight hours for a grandfather's body and mind to rebound from a fun-filled weekend with a rental car, and Wednesday night, you and your wife should be back to calling each other by your real names instead of your grandparent names, "Wah-Wee" and "Wah-Woo." Or, in our case, "Buh-Buh" and "Gaji."

By Thursday evening, things should be back to normal. You have a quiet dinner at home, just the two of you. There are no frozen waffles or macaroni and cheese in sight.

After dinner, you hold hands on the couch and talk about how this coming weekend you intend to relax and catch up on your reading. Maybe you'll even go to a movie that doesn't have any surfing penguins in it.

Then Friday afternoon your phone will ring. You will answer it and your daughter will tell you she has some great news. Her husband has to go to New York for a few days on business, and asked her to go with him.

At first she didn't think she could do it, but then she remembered how much fun you said you had with the grandbaby the past weekend, so why not try it again?

"Sure, honey, we'd love to," you say.

When you hang up, your wife sees the blank, vacant stare on your face. She asks what your daughter wanted.

When you answer with a numb "ungh," she gets the picture.

And the picture is drawn with crayons.

Five days later, you will go pick up your rental car once again.

But this time, you'll be sure to take the extra insurance.

SEVEN

DIFFERENT MUSCLES

Many of your grandfather friends will tell you that grandparenting involves an entirely different set of muscles from parenting.

Do not always believe what your friends tell you because they—like you—are old, and often have trouble distinguishing fact from fiction. Remember, these are the same friends who told you to dump your Microsoft shares, to never bet on the Red Sox, and that a colonoscopy can be a whole lot of fun.

The truth is, grandparenting and parenting take *exactly the same muscles*. Unfortunately, they are muscles that you gladly put into retirement when your youngest child stopped demanding piggyback rides at the age of eighteen.

Consider this:

When I ran the 100-yard dash in high school over forty years ago, I used my leg muscles for speed, my arm muscles for thrust and momentum, and my chest muscles to control my breathing. And often—as I approached the finish line—I would use my brain muscles to wonder, "Do they give a ribbon for finishing fifth?"

Today, the only way I could sprint 100 yards is if a bear or a rabid Scientologist were chasing me. Or a rabid Scientologist bear. I would also likely skedaddle if a magazine salesman knocked on my door and I recognized him as one

of my children. And since I can't move as fast as I used to, I'd probably end up with bear saliva on my backside and a lifetime subscription to *Field & Stream*. Still, I would've used exactly the same muscles I used back in high school. Just because I'm older, I would *not* have used my nose muscles to help me run. Or my tongue muscles to help me pump my arms. But I might have used my finger muscles to plug my ears so I didn't have to hear all about Tom and Katie's philosophies on child-rearing.

Because many grandfathers have forgotten what muscles and muscle groups they used as fathers, I'll go over some of them and compare how they are used in fatherhood versus grandfatherhood.

And remember, to young children, size *does* matter. But just because your waistline is twice the size it used to be, don't be fooled into thinking that you are twice as strong.

The Upper Arms and Shoulders

In fatherhood, these muscles were used for a wide variety of fun activities that usually began when your child was about nine months old. One of the most popular of these was taking your child under the arms and tossing him skyward. Then you'd watch as his eyes became as big as saucers and his arms opened reflexively, like a baby condor falling from his nest. He'd hold his breath, anticipating the rapid descent, and then would burst into uncontrollable and relieved laughter when you caught him. As a father, you were able to perform this move roughly forty-seven consecutive times, or until your child threw up on you.

In grandfatherhood, you will think that you can perform the same trick with your grandchild. But before you try, heed this warning: When you launch your grandchild upward, **DO NOT LET GO OF HIM!** Be sure to maintain constant contact with him on the way up and the way down.

There are a couple of important reasons for this.

First, if you toss him up while you're wearing your bifocals, you might see two of him, and catch the wrong one coming down. Second, if you throw the child so high that it takes a while for him to come down, you might forget what you did and walk away before he lands.

And unlike when you were younger, you'll only be able to perform four or five repetitions before you grab for your inhaler. You should not try to do more, unless you own stock in Advil or if you enjoy walking around for the next two weeks feeling like you have a flaming javelin stuck in your shoulder.

The Lower Back

Throughout fatherhood, these muscles were among the most important and useful muscles you possessed. It was the lower back that allowed a father to lean over a crib and kiss his beautiful baby good-night. It was also these muscles that helped you get out of bed six hours later to change her diaper, and spend the next hour and forty-five minutes holding her and pacing as you tried to get her to sleep, when all she wanted to do was play with your nose. And again, it was the lower back that permitted you to spring from your chair during a staff meeting the next morning when your boss yelled, "Hey, Kremski, is that you snoring?"

These muscles were also essential when you tried to secure your squirming thirty-pound angel into her car seat while she played with the dog. And they were even more important several hours later when you had to gently remove her from her car seat while she was asleep. And it was the lower back muscles that made your mouth muscles whisper, "How come this child weighs 30 pounds awake and 345 pounds asleep?"

And years later, as your children got older and greedier, it was your lower back muscles that helped you perfect the *Pocket Pivot*, a maneuver you used every time your children's hands moved anywhere near your wallet.

(Note: Once you become a grandfather, you will no longer need the Pocket Pivot. When your grandchild looks up at you with those amazingly beautiful eyes and says, "Grandpa, can I please have a dollar?" you will not give it to her. Instead, you will give her your wallet, your credit cards, your PIN, and any municipal bonds you have on hand.)

But now, with your children gone from home, you have tried to limit the non-recreational use of your lower back muscles to less strenuous duties like putting on your socks and picking up the remote control.

However, sometimes your wife will have other plans for these muscles—plans that involve unloading things like bags of groceries or sacks of potting soil from the trunk of her car. Hopefully, you've invested wisely enough to be able to have your groceries delivered and hire a gardener.

But when you have grandchildren, all of these muscles will be tested once again. When this happens, it is helpful to draw on what is known as *muscle memory*, a physiological phenomenon whereby muscles are able to remember and echo repeated actions. Unfortunately, by the time most of us become grandfathers, the only *muscle memory* we have is the memory of once having muscles. Because if we still had *true* muscle memory, how would we explain going out to our local golf course and shooting 92 one day and 148 the next?

But do not despair. I have unearthed a few devices to help you tone your muscles and get into "grandfather shape." Although I have used neither of these methods, both come highly recommended from some of my more creative grandfather friends. These exercises can be done in the comfort of your own home, thus protecting you from any urge to join a fitness center, where you would have to grunt, sweat, and try to hold in your stomach in front of all those young ladies who don't need to be at the gym in the first place.

First, I know many grandparents who enjoy a nice quiet beverage together at the end of their day. Whether you drink water or something stronger, this custom gives you an opportunity to relax after another busy day of playing dominoes or clipping coupons. For those of you who'd like to multi-task during your cocktail hour, you only need to go to your local sporting goods store and purchase a small, weighted wrist belt. However, you need not put this on your wrist, as these contraptions have been known to cause perspiration and, in some cases, a nasty little rash. Rather, you should attach the weighted belt to the bottom of your glass. However, if you are drinking a cocktail and you've chosen to load it down with an olive, onion, or cherry, be sure to reduce the weight in the belt accordingly. You don't want to overdo it. And no matter what your beverage of choice is, it's important that you sip slowly, thus performing enough reps to maximize the muscle restoration process.

The second option takes a little more work and is best suited to homes with high ceilings. First, have your local handyman build a three-foot-high platform in your kitchen, with a ramp leading to the summit. Second, recruit two neighborhood teenagers strong enough to bench press Rush Limbaugh, and ask them to place your refrigerator atop the platform. Voila! With the ramp at a fifteen-degree incline, you have created a wonderful apparatus that will build up your calves and thighs every time you sneak off for a snack.

This type of device will also serve you well in your bathroom, with your toilet bowl atop the platform. If you get up in the middle of the night as often as I do, it will work wonders for your cardiovascular system.

But for those of you who aren't exercise fanatics, there are some preventative steps you can take to lessen the muscle demands required of grandfatherhood.

Because you'll be belting your grandchild into a modern car seat, many of which are the size and weight of a lunar landing module, you may want to reconsider buying that hot, sexy little two-door convertible you and your wife have been eyeing to celebrate your last child finding his own address. Dealing with an infant's car seat in such a confined area will very likely put you in traction, so you might need a slightly larger vehicle.

With a wide-body Winnebago, you'll have plenty of room to secure your resistant grandchild into his safety seat without rupturing any vertebrae—his or yours. You'll also have plenty of extra room to tote all the high-tech equipment and gadgets that today's babies seem to require: Strollers that convert into one-room condos with Murphy beds, high chairs that fold into Volvos, and potty seats that come with headphones and plasma screens.

It's also a good idea to have several excuses handy that will explain why grandpas don't do certain recreational activities.

"Buh-Buh, get down on your hands and knees so we can play pony ride," pleaded my four-year-old granddaughter Alexandra.

"I'd like to, sweetheart," I said to her. "But I can't. I hurt my back in the war."

"You were in a war?" she asked, impressed. "Which one?"

"Yes, Buh-Buh," my wife said with a smug smile. "Which war was that again?" This was patently unfair, because Jill knew full well that during the height of the Vietnam "conflict" I somehow managed to spend my entire four-year enlistment at an Air Force base in western Massachusetts. That may sound cushy to some, but if you check your history books, you'll find that because of me, the strategic communities of Holyoke and Chicopee Falls remain free to this day. Jill also knows that my entire Air Force stint was spent as a clerk-typist. Our squadron motto was "We don't retreat! We backspace!"

I've learned that in situations like this, wives do not go out of their way to be overly helpful. That's because they're grand*ma*s and not grand*pa*s; and grand*ma*s are very rarely asked by their grandchildren to do things like wrestle or play pony ride. They may be asked to help the child draw a pony, or even to make cookies that are shaped like ponies; but sciatica-inducing pony rides seem to be grandpa territory.

Or so my wife thought until I turned the tables on her.

"Maybe Grandma would like to play pony ride with you," I suggested to Alexandra. "She wasn't in a war."

Alexandra looked up at Jill. "Can *you* give me a pony ride, Grandma?"

Jill stared at me. It's the look she uses whenever I outwit her. I remembered seeing it only once before, about twenty years ago.

"I can't," she told Alexandra. "I hurt my back, too."

"How?" the girl demanded.

"How?" Jill answered, noticing that I was waiting for her answer as well. "Well, I hurt it when I had to carry around your poor old grandfather after his war injury."

Alexandra's eyes lit up with admiration. And then the two of them headed off to the kitchen to make cookies that looked like ponies.

EIGHT

COMMUNICATION ARTS

Social scientists have suggested that couples who have been together for many years sometimes take on some of their partners' traits. These scientists further suggest that in some cases, couples of grandparent age may actually begin to look like each other. I hope and pray that this is not in store for my wife, who is considered by all to be a beautiful and refined woman. But I'm sure this assessment would change should she start becoming more like me, sprouting neck hair and scratching herself in public.

Another thing that changes with long-time couples is the way they communicate. I've observed that as we get older, my wife and I seem to have less to say to each other. This is not because we love each other less or care about each other less. Quite the opposite. It is because, as grandparents, we usually have fewer things to talk about than we did when we were younger. Things like our young children, our jobs, or disco. And because we spend most of our waking hours together, it follows that—should something exciting happen in your life—like your SecureHorizons health plan announcing that it will begin covering tummy tucks, it's likely to happen to the both of you, which means there's not much to talk about, because you were both there in the first place.

Because you spend so much time together, it's highly unlikely that while you and your wife are watching a special on the Spanish Inquisition that you will turn to her and say, "Darn, honey, I almost forgot. Did I tell you that, while you were volunteering at the hospital yesterday, I had lunch with Antonio Banderas? He ordered the paella."

As further evidence that older couples talk less, I want you to recall the last time you and your wife were in a restaurant, and a younger couple sitting nearby had to call over to your table, "Hey, you two think you could pipe down a little?"

There's another reason people who have been together a long time speak to each other less. We've developed our own personal shorthand. We need fewer words to get our message across.

Think back to a cold winter night twenty-five years or so ago. It's nearly 11:30, and your children are all fast asleep; and when you snuggle up to your wife, there's a lot more than dreams of sugarplums dancing though your head. You gently put your arms around her and kiss her neck, complimenting her on her perfume. You even say how lovely she looks in that full-length flannel nightgown. When she hears that, she knows where you're headed.

"Sweetie, I'd love to, but I am absolutely exhausted, plus it's my morning to drive carpool tomorrow, so I have to get up even earlier to make the kids' lunches. Night, honey. I love you."

Then she kisses you, clicks the remote, and hands it to you. As she rolls over for her short trip to slumberland, at least you hear a comforting voice:

"And now . . . Heeeeeeerrre's Johnny!"

But now that you're of grandfather age, the same situation might very well go like this:

"Honey?" you say sweetly.

"Get real," she says.

So you grab the remote and switch on *Antiques Roadshow.* Shorthand.

But you will learn that when a grandchild enters your life, much of your shorthand will disappear faster than free meatballs at Bingo Night.

Here's how it goes where I live. . . .

Because it's just the two of us at home, when I hear car keys jingling, I react like Pavlov's dog. I know it means that Jill is about to leave the house.

"Where are you off to?" I ask, already knowing her answer.

"Out," is all she ever chooses to tell me. And these days, it seems she very rarely requests the pleasure of my company.

And I am fine with this, because the places wives go when they go *out* are not usually places husbands want to go.

And though I don't know exactly where *out* is, I do know that when Jill does go *out*, it often involves spending a fair amount of money on things like the new microwave she recently bought. I also know where Jill's out *isn't.* Experience has taught me that *out* isn't anywhere near the do-it-yourself-doggie wash, the self service car wash, or any other place that would require Jill to do something that she has determined I should do.

We both think this is a fine arrangement.

But not long ago, a brush salesman knocked on my door.

"Hello," said the thirty-year-old man wearing a cheap tie and a white shirt with a collar two sizes larger than his neck. "Is your wife home?"

"No, she's out," I said, wanting to get back to the kitchen and the new microwave. When he knocked, I had just started nuking a pepperoni pizza, which is an illegal substance when Jill is home, as she claims the smell makes her nauseous. But since Jill's nose went out with her, it will not be affended.

"When will she be home?" the brush salesman asked.

"I don't know," I responded impatiently.

"You don't know?" This young man apparently found it inconceivable that a husband wouldn't know where his wife was, or when she was coming home. He probably suspected Jill was holed up inside, hiding from him behind the sofa. "Where did she go?" he asked, looking in suspiciously.

"Out," I told him.

"Out where?"

"I dunno. *Out* out." My voice rose slightly because the microwave beeped, letting me know that my frozen pizza would be ready as soon as I added my customary three pounds of Parmesan.

"Are you telling me that your wife went out and you don't know where she is?" he asked, appalled at meeting such a dunderheaded, negligent husband. I could tell this was no longer simply about brushes.

I noticed a wedding ring on his finger. "How long have you been married?" I asked.

"Two years," he said proudly.

I chuckled. "I suppose you know exactly where your wife goes when she goes out."

"Yes, I do," he said, doing his best to make me feel ashamed.

"Good," I said. "Then go wherever that is, and my wife is probably nearby. Have a nice day."

But when our grandchild is visiting and I hear the keys jingling in the other room, I don't even have to ask where Jill is going, because I will soon know the complete itinerary.

"Oh, you look so sweet!" I hear her say to Claire, our six-month-old granddaughter. Keep in mind that Claire barely understands two words: "bottle" and "more." But that doesn't stop Jill from throwing our shorthand right out the window and suddenly becoming an AARP tour guide.

"We are going to have such fun today!" Jill says to Claire, depositing her into her $20,000, 8-cylinder stroller. "And we have sooo much to do! First, we have to go to the market and pick up things for dinner. Then, we'll stop at the bakery on Elm and buy a pie for dessert. It's right next door to the dry cleaners, so we'll stop there and pick up Buh-Buh's shirt that he spilled pasta sauce all over." Claire chuckled at that. It seems my eating mishaps bring joy to everyone's life.

"Then we'll go to Baby World," Jill continued, "so we can get you a new outfit before we have your six-month picture taken at the mall! On our way home, we'll go visit my friend Mady so she can see what a beautiful little girl you are, okay?"

Then something even more unexpected came out of Jill's mouth: "Want to go with us, Buh-Buh?"

"What?" I thought. "Me? She asked me to go *out*?" I briefly considered it, but then I remembered that I had plans for when Jill was out. Big plans.

I was about to beg off when I saw Claire smiling up at me with a smile that said, "C'mon, go with us. You can hold me while Gaji shops, and I promise I won't spit up in your shirt pocket like I did in church."

"I'll be ready in five minutes," I said. As I hurried upstairs, I noticed my stomach bouncing with each step I took. That was all the proof I needed to convince me that scrapping my original plan was definitely the right decision. That other frozen pepperoni pizza would be much better off without me.

NINE

THE VERDICT? NOT GUILTY!

As fun and as rewarding as grandchildren can be, and as much as I strive to be a perfect grandfather, there was one development I did not anticipate. When it happens to you—and happen it will—it will likely hit you like a brick. It's not pretty, but it's inevitable; and even the most dedicated and loving grandfather will have to deal with it.

"It" occurs most frequently after your grandchild has reached the age of four and has more energy than a twelve-pack of Red Bull. And "it" often coincides with the first time you take care of her for longer than a weekend without her parents lurking to make sure that you feed her properly, get her to bed on time, and promise to watch your language while she's around.

For those of you who haven't yet soloed with your post-toddler grandchild, you should know that this takes mounds of preparation. I hope my experience will be helpful.

The first thing we did was to contact everyone we know (some of whom we haven't spoken to since the Eisenhower administration) to casually let them know—should they get the urge to call us to get together—that we were not available the following week.

"We'll be too wonderfully busy tending to our beautiful grandchild," we told them. "What? You didn't know we had a grandchild? Oh, I know we look way too young for that, but it's true. If you don't believe us, go to our website, www.coolestgrandparentsonthisoranyotherplanet.org."

The next thing we did was check with the child's mother to find out what supplies and provisions we'd need for the week. In addition to items like No More Tears shampoo and Mr. Bubble bath foam, she said that our granddaughter liked frozen waffles, bologna, white bread, mayonnaise, creamy peanut butter, pizza in a pocket, and several different brands of sugared cereal.

And finally, she said firmly, "But no junk food."

After renting a U-Haul to get the groceries home, I decided to make up another list: things to do with our granddaughter for the five days she'd be with us. I wanted the week to be perfect, so I settled on the beach, Disneyland, the San Diego Zoo, and a G-rated movie.

I figured that should be enough for Day One.

When Friday afternoon rolled around, I'd done everything on my list—and then some—to make sure everything was perfect for our little angel's arrival. I even spent two hours studying our television's instruction manual so I could program the remote to automatically locate Nickelodeon and the Disney Channel. But when I still couldn't figure it out, Jill asked the nine-year-old from next door come over. It took her less then three minutes.

When she saw my expression of inadequacy, the little girl did her best to make me feel better.

"It's okay, Mr. M.," she said. "My grandpa doesn't know how to do this either. And he's younger than you."

"Oh? How old is he?"

"Eighty-three, I think. Bye!"

By Friday evening, the two of us were so excited that we peeked through the front drapes every time we heard a car approaching. Where are they? They said they'd drop her off at 5:30, and it's already 5:35. How irresponsible and inconsiderate of them! When they finally did pull into our driveway, we tackled each other trying to be the first out the door to get to our granddaughter.

As we unloaded her things from the car, our son-in-law said he'd like to use the bathroom. When he tried to get out of the car, I pushed him back in and told him he'd have to wait; there was a very clean restroom at a nearby gas station.

Have a nice weekend, kids! Bye-bye!

And as they drove off in an SUV the size of our first apartment, we held our granddaughter's hand and hoped that maybe they'd decide to extend their five-day getaway to six . . . or maybe even seven.

But they stuck to their schedule. In fact, they returned an hour early. And when they put our granddaughter into her car seat, she told them that she had "the most funnest time ever!"

That made us feel very good.

And as they drove away, we stood and waved good-bye. As Jill continued waving her hand like a beauty queen in a parade, I glanced at her, expecting to see a tear or two. But instead, I saw a pair of eyes that looked exactly like Wile E. Coyote's after he's been steamrolled by the Road Runner. I suspected that I had that look, too, but I was too exhausted to lift a mirror to check.

Once their car was out of sight, we turned to each other and immediately realized that we both shared the same terrible thought. But how could that be? We love our granddaughter more than life itself.

Then why were we so happy to see her go?

What kind of grandparents are we?

An hour after they left, we were still beating ourselves up for feeling so good that our little angel was back where she belonged. Finally, we decided that if we were going to continue to chew on our own guilt, it might taste better combined with some Chinese food.

And it was while we were in the restaurant waiting for our "to go" order that we first saw her: the mysterious woman we still refer to as "Our Lady of Fung Lum's."

She was a bit older and was standing by herself as she perused the menu; I could tell she was having a tough time deciding what to order.

Finally, she approached Jill. "Excuse me, dear," she asked in an Irish accent thicker than a pint of warm Guinness, "but have you had the orange chicken here before?"

"I have," I said. "It's terrific."

"Thank you. I think my husband will enjoy that. He was going to come with," she said. "But he couldn't get out of his chair."

"Bad back?" I asked.

"No, exhaustion," she said with a laugh. "We had our grandchildren for a few days and they just left. Jesus, Mary, Joseph . . . peace and quiet at last."

Hearing this, we sensed that here was someone who would understand our pain. After she placed her order, we told her about our last five days. She listened patiently with an experienced smile.

"I'm sure your granddaughter is a beautiful girl," she said, sensing how we felt. "My four are absolute angels," she continued. "We love them dearly and would do anything for them. But that doesn't mean we want them around every minute, now does it?"

My wife and I exchanged relieved glances.

"It's like taking a vacation abroad," the lady continued. "Every sight you see is more wonderful than the last. You love every moment of your trip. But after a while, you start missing your own home. But that doesn't mean you didn't like your trip, now does it? No. It's just time for your bonnet to be hanging on your own hat rack."

Jill looked at me and smiled. Her Wile E. Coyote eyes were gone.

"Our grandchildren stay with us often, and we always enjoy it when they do," the lady said. "But every time their parents come to pick them up, I think of a little poem I heard years ago."

And then she recited in her delightful brogue:

> *I've seen the lights of Paris.*
> *I've seen the lights of Rome.*
> *But the most beautiful lights I've ever seen*
> *Are the taillights of the grandchildren going home.*

As we laughed at this, we were told that our order was ready. We paid the bill and started out, feeling 1,000% better than when we walked in.

"It was wonderful talking to you," we said to our new Irish friend as we opened the door to leave.

"Likewise. And I hope you enjoy a nice, quiet dinner," she said.

Same to you, Our Lady of Fung Lum's.

Same to you.

TEN

SPARE THE ROD . . .

I've learned that the difference between how I disciplined my own children versus how I discipline my grandchildren is not unlike the difference between taking a shower by myself or taking one with my Great Aunt Flossie. The first occurs daily, but the other will only happen if the future of mankind depends on it. And with global warming, super-sizing, and cheese sauces, how much time do I really have anyway?

I recall that I rarely disciplined my own children before they reached the age of eighteen months—unless they did something seriously wrong—like hit one of their siblings with a croquet mallet, used the contents of their diapers for finger paints, or made fun of my haircut.

Disciplining begins around this age because this is normally when a child begins to learn the concept of right and wrong. Not coincidentally, it is also just after he has learned that by standing up and walking like you do, he can get from *Point A* to *Point B* faster than he can on his knees. And often, he can also get there a lot faster than you can, which is why most trouble is located at *Point B*. Because if a child could break something valuable at *Point A*, there'd be no reason to go to *Point B* in the first place.

Your advantage as a grandfather is that you've learned this and a lot more during your years as a father. But your grandchild's parents have yet to learn it and probably don't know that you already know it, because they still believe that their parents don't know much of anything. And it won't be until your grandchild is about eleven—and causing them to consider auctioning him off on eBay—that they'll realize how much you do know, *and* that you've known it all along.

And all that learning comes from your experience as a father. There is nothing more important for a grandfather than experience, except perhaps having a prostate smaller than an overripe mango. And one of the many things experience has taught you is that while it's very difficult to discipline your *child* before she's eighteen months old, it's even more difficult to discipline your *grandchild* before she's, say, forty-five.

And why is this? Because we want our grandchildren to like us. Back when you were a parent, you didn't expect your children to like you. In fact, they weren't *supposed* to like you, unless they also liked going to bed earlier than they thought they should, studying as much as you insisted, and having you drop them off at school and giving them a big good-bye kiss in front of their friends.

The only parents who worried about their children liking them were the zany few who claimed, "I want to be my child's best friend." Do you know who I wanted to be my children's best friend? The straight-A student who lived three doors down, with a school teacher mother and a Marine drill sergeant father. What's more, this family also had a dog trained to sniff out a) illegal substances and b) socks that have been worn to school more than six days in a row.

So whether our children liked us or not, they were stuck with us. We hoped that if we loved them and nurtured them while they were growing up, maybe they'd find time to like us later on.

But because we so desperately want our grandchildren to think we're the greatest thing since SpongeBob SquarePants, we have trouble disciplining them.

I don't know any grandmother who has ever threatened a grandchild with, "You just wait till your grandfather gets home!" There are a couple of simple reasons for this. First, grandfathers are usually home to begin with; and second, a grandmother knows that rather than disciplining his grand-daughter, a grandfather will instead say that *all* children misbehave sometimes, then give his beautiful four-year-old granddaughter a crisp five-dollar bill.

Let's look at two common scenarios where virtually everything is the same except for one thing. In the first, think back to when you were a young dad. It's 12:30, Friday night, and you and your wife of six years come home after a rare night out with friends. Your babysitter tells you that your one-and-a-half-year-old was a perfect angel.

"She went to sleep without any complaining at all," she tells you. Then she adds, "Your baby is definitely the sweetest and smartest child I have ever been around in my whole life."

You're thrilled with this assessment, even though your sitter is only fifteen, and hasn't been around many children because a) she is an only child, and b) she is home schooled. (A few years later, you'll learn that she left home—and therefore, school—to pursue her lifelong dream of becoming a magician's assistant.)

After driving your sitter home, you and your wife get to bed around one. When she yawns, you try to win some romantic points by hugging her and volunteering to get up with the baby in the morning so she can sleep in. And though she is thankful, your only reward is a tender good-night kiss and instructions to make sure your daughter eats all her cereal for breakfast.

The next morning, you hear your daughter stirring in her room at 6:30. At 6:31, you go back to sleep. At 6:42, you hear her whimpering. At 6:43, you go back to sleep. At 6:45, your wife elbows you . . . hard. At 6:45:05, you decide it would be a good time to get up with the baby.

After changing your daughter's diaper with your eyes half open, you stumble into the kitchen and deposit her in her high chair. Then you go to the refrigerator and grab breakfast for both of you: cereal and milk for her; a slice of three-day old sausage pizza and a half-empty quart bottle of soda for you. You set her cereal and milk on her tray, and just in case your enormously gifted child is unsure about what to do with the cereal, you rub your tummy and say "Mmm, mmm."

She looks at you curiously, then says, "Naaahhh." And as you slug down the flat Mountain Dew, she pushes the cereal off her tray and onto the floor.

You can't believe it. Your little angel has never done anything like that before! What did that maverick home-schooler teach her?

So while your dog thinks he's hit the jackpot and happily laps up the spillage, you go and get another bowl. When you open the pantry for more cereal, your daughter spots something in there.

"Geh-tee-oh," she yells, pointing to a can of SpaghettiO's.

Although you think that's very cute, you also know your duties as a father.

"Honey, SpaghettiO's are not for breakfast."

"Geh-tee-oh!" she insists.

"No, sweetie, you have cereal for breakfast," you tell her as you place another full bowl in front of her.

"No! Geh-tee-oh," she yells. And then she pushes the second bowl onto the floor.

You stare at your daughter. She looks at you defiantly, and then gives you that strained, red-faced look that indicates that her defiance has taken the form of her soiling her just-changed diaper.

"Geh-tee-oh!"

So there you are: Two gunfighters in the old West. High noon, Main Street.

But you're the sheriff of this town. You know what you have to do, even though you hate to do it.

"Throwing cereal is a bad girl," you tell her, trying to sound stern. Then you take her tiny hand in yours and give your hand a firm smack, a move fathers know is like throwing marshmallows at a man in full body armor.

She looks at you, stunned at the sound, and her eyes become as big as Frisbees. She wants to cry, but she can't, because her lungs won't allow her to let out any air while she curls her quivering lower lip. (This is a move that she'll learn to perfect as she gets older, and will usually employ when the discussion involves boyfriends, curfews, or how that dent got in your car.) When she's finally able to exhale, it's a good one. That's because all of that retained air produces a scream that would make Howard Dean proud. Glasses shatter. Dogs run for cover. Except your dog, who's happily slurping up his second bowl of milk and cereal and trying to remember why he was so jealous when you first brought this little creature home.

"Waaaaaaaahhhhh!"

And although you know you did the right thing, you feel terrible about it. You remove your wailing daughter from her high chair and hold her.

"There, there. It's okay, honey. Daddy didn't mean it."

"Waaaaaaaahhhhh!"

"What did you do?!" demands a sleepy, unhappy voice.

You turn to see your wife glaring at you. The dog also sees her and cowers under the table. Sometimes it's good to be a dog.

"Well . . ." you start to explain.

"It's all right, sweetie," she says to the baby as she takes her from you. Then she takes a whiff of your daughter's diaper. "Doesn't Daddy know how to change a diaper?"

You start to explain, but before you can get a word out, your wife says to the baby, "Don't worry, honey. Mommy's here now."

Then she and your daughter disappear, leaving you alone with the dog, who determines that it's safe to return to his milk and cereal.

You sit and worry that your beautiful daughter will hate you forever. But a few hours later when you're sadly watching your alma mater's football team get pummeled, your cereal-tossing daughter toddles in, just when the other team scores another touchdown, making it 1,770 to 3.

"Oh no," you say. "This is horrible."

"That's okay, Daddy," she says, climbing onto your lap. "*I* love you."

Then she gives you a big kiss.

And the world is a wonderful place to be.

Now, I want you to look at the same scenario twenty-five years later. You are now the *grandfather* of an eighteen-month-old.

Once again it's Friday night. But instead of a late night out with friends, you and your wife are at home yawning and playing Scrabble. It's 9:30. The game has taken a little longer than normal because the outcome will determine who gets up with your granddaughter in the morning. It's your final turn, as you hold the two remaining letters. Your wife has a twenty-point lead and smiles at you victoriously. But just as you're ready to concede defeat, you see it: a place for your *Q-U*! You put it in front of the word "ILL" and you win!

You spring to your feet, do some nifty dance moves, and cheer. You see the defeat in your wife's eyes.

"Oh, pipe down," she says. "You'll wake your granddaughter."

You glide over and kiss her. "It's okay, sweetie, maybe next time," you gloat. "But tomorrow? *I* get to get up with her!"

The next morning, you and your granddaughter are enjoying breakfast together. She is on her second helping as you force your way through your bowl of cholesterol-lowering oatmeal and skim milk.

You hear your wife approaching. "Mornin', darling," you call.

"Good morning, love," she says. Then she looks at her granddaughter in her high chair.

"My goodness!" she asks. "What is that all over her?"

You look at your perfectly happy granddaughter, whose angelic face is covered with tomato sauce and noodles.

"SpaghettiO's," you tell her.

"SpaghettiO's? For breakfast? Where did she get an idea like that?"

"It's what she wanted," you tell her.

"Oh," says your wife. "Well, then, give me a bowl, too."

ELEVEN

WHEN THE LITTLE HAND IS ON THE SEVEN

Like most grandfathers whose children have been out of the house for a while, and who have shown no desire to return for any period longer than a Sunday dinner, I have thoroughly "de-childrened" our home. This means that once again I can use the bathroom at any time without needing a reservation or a book of matches, I can now open a bottle of aspirin without requiring the Jaws of Life to remove the childproof cap, and I can spend an entire day at home without once hearing the word "dude."

I'm sure it didn't take you and your wife very long to get back into the routine of "just the two of you," which opened up a world that you had almost forgotten about, a world where weekends are yours again. Now you can start out with some nice Saturday morning lounging, some brisk Saturday afternoon exercise, and some soothing Saturday evening Aleve.

I have a friend who is a board-certified Emergency Room Physician. His real name is Michael, but everyone—co workers included, calls him "Zip." Now although this may be an endearing nickname, it is not one that I'd like to hear if I were brought into the ER because, say, I was hit by a car. "Don't worry, Mr. Milligan," the nurse says to me as I begin to lose consciousness. "You're lucky this happened tonight. Dr. Zip is here." I don't know about you, but I like my doctors to be named Arthur, Carl, or Edward.

Despite his nickname, Zip is an extremely intelligent and responsible man. Yet, within a week after his children moved out of the house, he called me and proclaimed, "This is great! We can do anything, even run around the house in our underwear if we want!"

I'd heard men use that expression before, but had never really given it any thought. But now, I suddenly had mental pictures—and not pretty ones—of my doctor friend running around his house in his skivvies. Thankfully, I have never seen Zip cavorting in his underpants and unless hell is even worse than it's cracked up to be, I never will. But just the thought of him in his living room, pirouetting around tables and somersaulting over sofas in his Fruit of the Looms is evidence enough that grandfathers having the freedom to run around in their underwear is not a good thing. And that it should not be guaranteed by the Constitution.

I am not ashamed to say that I don't like to *run* anywhere, unless it's really extremely urgent, like if I pull into the Denny's parking lot at 4:59, knowing the Senior Dinner Discount stops at 5:00. Also, I've recently discovered that when I run anywhere at my age, my belly button arrives at my destination about three minutes before I do. But even if I did enjoy a good run now and then, I would surely not do it in my underwear. And while I would certainly welcome the opportunity to watch my beautiful wife run around our house in *her* underwear, I think that's about as likely to happen as Britney Spears opening a chain of driving schools.

But whether you like to run around the house in your U-Trou, or just sit and enjoy the quiet, you will have to make some adjustments to your tranquil lifestyle now that you have grandchildren. One of the first changes you'll have to make is to your alarm clock.

You won't be needing it.

When we were younger and had jobs that required us to be at work on time, we often chose to ignore the alarm clock. That is why many of us often showed up for work with hair like Donald Trump's and breath like Donald Duck's.

But now that we're older—and in many cases, don't have to be anywhere at any particular hour—we set our alarms for earlier, which means we have much more time to do much less. This explains why so many men of grandfather age take up time-filling hobbies like gardening, golf, and eating dinner at 2:30 in the afternoon.

But you will learn that no matter what time you wake up in the morning, your grandchild will be awake at least a half-hour earlier.

And although a grandchild will tiptoe into your room while you're sleeping, she will not immediately wake you. That is because before her parents dropped her off for their romantic weekend getaway, they told her, "Grandma and Grandpa are old. Let them sleep until they wake up. And if they don't wake up by 9:30, hold a mirror under their noses like I showed you. Then call 911."

And while your granddaughter won't wake you, what she *will* do is hold her breath and put her face about one millimeter from yours while you sleep. But soon, unless she has the lungs of a Japanese pearl diver, she will begin breathing as she waits for you to open your eyes.

It won't be long before you become aware that someone is very close to you, and that her unique breath has the unmistakable aroma of a youngster who hasn't yet learned the value of a toothbrush. It's now that you have a critical decision to make. You can keep your eyes closed and pretend you're still in a deep slumber, hoping this will buy you a few more minutes of sleep while she loses interest. You should know, however, that most grandchildren can wait out Rip Van Winkle.

Or you may try to peek, opening your eyes a micrometer, thinking your grandchild will not notice. But before you attempt this, be warned that grandchildren have the eyes of a hawk, and that a hawk can see a gopher blink from 1,000 feet. So unless you've always wanted to be an airsick gopher, keep your eyes closed.

Probably the best course of action is for you to open your eyes as wide as you can and pretend you've been awake for an hour. Then say to your granddaughter, "Good morning, beautiful. How did you sleep?!"

"Good," she says. "Can we play Uncle Wiggly now?"

As you try to remember what she's talking about, you recall that last night you played so many games of Uncle Wiggly that you never want to see his chubby cheeks or cutesy overalls again. In fact, because of your years of endlessly playing this simplistic board game with your own children, you have developed a serious dislike for Uncle Wiggly, and uncles in general.

Last night she had asked, "Just one more game, grandpa? Please?"

"You have to go to bed, honey," you said. (Note: This is grandfather-speak for, "*I* have to go to bed, honey.")

"Okay. But can we play Uncle Wiggly again in the morning?" she asked.

"Sure," you said.

"Promise?"

> **CAUTION:** *The Surgeon Grandfather has determined that saying "Promise" to a grandchild can have serious consequences.*

You should use this word only if you mean it. Do not use it as freely as you did with your own children, when you could wiggle out of promises by re-promising.

"Daddy, can we go to JollyLand next Saturday?"

"Sure."

"Promise?"

"Promise."

Then when you got home from work on Friday night, you had to break the bad news. "Kids, we can't go to JollyLand tomorrow. I have to work."

"But you promised us!"

"Yes, I did. But long before I promised you that, I promised your mother that we would always live in a nice house. And that our house would have a roof and would not be attached to a pick-up truck."

"But Daddy . . ."

"We'll go next weekend. Promise."

"Okay, but we get to stay until it closes, okay?"

"Promise."

This ploy does not work with a grandchild, because a grandchild does not accept negotiation. Instead, if you break a promise, she will break off all discussion and look at you with a hurt and disappointment that you haven't seen since her hamster got out of his cage and you accidentally backed over it with your car.

But even then, you were able to save the day (but unfortunately, not the hamster) by telling her that little Herbie wasn't dead, just a little sick. And then you told her that when she went in for her nap, you would go to the pet store and get a secret hamster medicine that only smart grandpas know about. And when she wakes up, Herbie will be just fine.

"Promise?" she asked.

"Promise," you promised.

And sure enough, when she woke up from her nap and ran out to her hamster cage, there was Herbie, looking fit as a fiddle, although she did mention that he seemed a teensy bit chubbier.

"That's because the medicine makes him look a little fatter," you explained.

"You mean like your medicine?" she asked.

Back at your bedside, your granddaughter continues, "C'mon, Grandpa let's play Uncle Wiggly. You promised."

"All right, honey," you say as you pull yourself out of bed. "But first I think someone needs to brush their teeth."

"You're right, Grandpa," she says, sensing an odor. "But hurry up. And don't wake Grandma."

TWELVE

GRANDCHILD PROOFING

In addition to your alarm clock, I can tell you with confidence that there are several other things in your house that you will not be using when your grandchildren visit. I am not suggesting that you need to hide these things from your grandchildren, but you may want to hide them from yourself so you aren't constantly reminded how much you miss them.

Bathroom Reading Material

If your grandchildren stay with you for an extended period of time, which means longer than, say, three hours and forty-five minutes, you will have to put your normal routine on hold until they are on their way home again. Although you know that your young grandchildren are beautiful, intelligent and all kinds of wonderful, you'll learn that there's another thing they are: *there*. And when they are *there*, it seems their favorite place to be is wherever you are.

It's no revelation that older men put a high value on proper bathroom time. It's as much a part of our lives as food, clothing, and talking back to the television set. But finding quiet time when your grandchildren visit is very difficult, if not impossible. You have to learn to pick your spots, like when you see your wife and granddaughter

watching a video with a singing starfish. This is a good time to make your move because your wife is nodding off and your granddaughter is transfixed to the screen, even though she's been watching this video almost non-stop since she arrived. So you make your exit, newspaper folded under your arm.

You enter the bathroom and shut the door very quietly.

As you get ready to catch up on what's been going on in the world since your grandchild arrived, you listen very closely. The only sound you hear is your wife and granddaughter singing in the distance, "*I'm Sam the Starfish, that's who I am. I live in the ocean with Calvin the Clam!*"

But as you sit and unfold the newspaper, don't think you're in the clear. Soon, you hear the doorknob turn. But it won't open, since one of the things you learned from years of being a father is to always lock the bathroom door. And to store your wallet on a high dresser where no little people could reach it.

"Grandpa, are you in there?" your granddaughter calls through the door.

You know that your best bet is to remain silent.

"Yes, honey, I'm in here."

"Can I come in?"

"No, darling, you can't."

"Why?"

"Uh, just because. But I'll be out soon," you lie.

"What are you doing?" she asks.

You know that she knows exactly what you are doing. She has a bathroom at home. She knows what she does in there, and what her parents do in there. But, like lawyers, grandchildren enjoy asking questions they already know the answers to.

That's why they ask things like, "Isn't Grandma pretty?" "Do you want a back rub?" "Can I have a kiss?"

You decide that since she already knows what you're doing in the bathroom, there's no reason to be anything less than honest.

"What am I doing? I'm re-grouting the tile."

She has no idea what that means. So of course she says, "Really? Can I help?"

"I don't think so, honey. It's a very dangerous job," you tell her.

"That's okay, grandpa. I'm not afraid."

"I know you're not afraid. But are you certified?"

"What's that?"

"Certified. It means do you have enough education to re-grout tile?"

She thinks for a moment, then says, "I know my colors."

"What about math? What's two plus seven?"

There's a worried pause, then, "A million?"

"Well, I guess you *are* qualified. Yes, you can help. We'll start tomorrow."

"Promise?"

Careful now, Grandpa.

Your Golf Clubs

When your grandchildren are visiting for the weekend, you will not have time to play golf. You probably won't have time to watch golf, either. In fact, you'll be lucky to find time to even spell "golf."

If you don't believe me, just try running it by your wife.

"Honey, I know the grandkids are coming tomorrow, but rather than spending the entire day with all of you, I thought I'd take a little break—only five or six hours—to play some golf with Ernie and the guys while you and the four grandchildren go to the zoo, then grocery shopping. What do you say?"

When you regain consciousness and the attending physician asks you how your four iron found its way to that particular part of your body, my advice to you is to plead ignorance.

The Rules to Any Board or Card Game

Grandchildren want to win in everything they do. And no matter how hard you try to make sure that happens, following the rules can often get in the way. So unless you want them to like their other grandpa—the one with all the money and the winter home in Aspen—more than they like you, roll with it.

Any Deck with All 52 Cards

See above.

Ambien or Any Sleep Aid

Unless you live in a jet engine testing facility, when your grandchildren visit you will need absolutely nothing to help you get to sleep at bedtime. And to grandfathers, "bedtime" means any time after *Oprah*. Not only will you not need to take a pill, at the end of the day you will not have enough strength to open the bottle or to lift a glass of water to your mouth.

THIRTEEN

"NOT TONIGHT, GRANDPA"

When I recall my own grandparents, many wonderful and lasting images and memories pop into my head: holiday dinners, old-smelling furniture, and stories about how they were so poor during the Great Depression that, even on the sunniest day, their family of seventeen could only afford one shadow. But when I think of my grandparents, there's one thing I have never thought about: sex.

And if any of *you* think of your grandparents in this way, you need to put down this book immediately and contact a licensed therapist.

It was difficult enough accepting that our *parents* were not always sleeping when they were in their bedroom. But our grandparents? Grandparents didn't have sex.

Well, today they do.

Or so I'm told.

And one of the reasons that grandmothers and grandfathers are smiling more these days? Viagra. This and similar medications have helped more grandfathers get back in the saddle than a Sun City riding instructor. Yet no one I talked to would admit that he ever once needed the assistance of these supplements, so I can only assume that either the sales figures for these products have been enormously inflated, or that my family, friends, and colleagues are lying through their dentures while looking at life through blue-tinted glasses.

It seems that the average man is very uneasy discussing such a matter, probably because he thinks he's the only guy on earth who suffers from occasional power outages. But if that were the case, why would pharmaceutical companies spend so much money promoting their products?

And it should be no surprise that the manufacturers of these items spend a good deal of their advertising dollars on televised sporting events—particularly golf—which is watched overwhelmingly by middle-aged men.

After extensive research, I can tell you without qualification that you will never see a Viagra commercial air during *Dora the Explorer*, or a Levitra spot featuring a recently-satisfied, gorgeous older couple during an episode of *Pimp My Ride*.

So why golf? Probably because it's a sport in which older men can still participate and feel competitive with other older men. All one has to do is be able to sit in a cart without falling out more than twice a round, hit a ball that's not moving, remember where it went, get back in the cart, ride another fifteen feet, and hit it again. The game's most difficult aspect is being clever enough to avoid paying for drinks afterwards.

Arguably, one of the most talented and admired athletes in any sport is New York Yankees shortstop Derek Jeter. But I think it's a safe bet that, after watching a baseball game where he has made one spectacular play after another, very few grandfathers jump off the sofa and say to their wives, "Honey, let's go outside so you can you hit me some grounders. I want to work on my double play move."

Or after watching an NFL game, we're not likely to shout out, "I'll be back in an hour, sweetie. I'm going down to the high school to lay some big licks on a tackling dummy."

But golf is different. When Tiger Woods wins yet another tournament, practice ranges are immediately stacked three-deep with grandfather-aged men who should know better than to go out in public dressed like that.

Erectile dysfunction (ED) is not like most medical conditions, where you need a doctor to tell you you've got it. You already know you've got it, and not only that, you remember the exact moment when you first learned you'd got it.

Also, it is not an affliction that anyone else would be aware that you have, unless you told someone—which is about as likely to happen as Keith Richards becoming a spokesman for a line of skin care products.

For example, if you suddenly started growing a second nose from your forehead, it would be obvious something was wrong with you; anyone might be tempted to stop you on the street and say, "Sir, your upper nose is running and it's dripping unpleasant-looking goo into your eye. Perhaps you should talk to a doctor about that."

That would be easy; but talking to a doctor about ED is an entirely different and uncomfortable proposition. So I dealt with it the way most men would: I put it off as long as possible. But my wife and I were celebrating our wedding anniversary in a week, and we have this long-standing tradition. So to speak.

Obviously, handling this over the phone would be far less humiliating, so after a few false starts I finally worked up the courage to call my doctor's office.

"Good morning, Dr. Funderbin's office. Danielle speaking."

"Shoot," I thought to myself. "Danielle!" She's the perky twenty-five-year-old who greets me with an attractive smile each time I make an office visit. Over time, I've managed to delude myself into thinking that she's harboring a harmless crush on me. This makes her the last person I want to know about my "problem."

"How may I help you?" Danielle asked.

"Yes," I said, lowering my voice at least twelve octaves. "I'd like to speak with Dr. Funderbin."

"What is the call regarding?" she asked.

"It's about a prescription," I told her in a voice so low that I sounded like Weezy from *The Jeffersons*.

"Is it for a sore throat?" Danielle asked helpfully. "You sound like you have a cold."

"No, it's not a cold. Could I please just speak to Dr. Funderbin?"

"He's with patients all morning. But if you like, I could put you through to his personal voice mail."

"Fine."

"Okay, I'll connect you. Leave a message and Melanie, his nurse, will call you back by the end of the day."

"Whoa!" I said, my voice involuntarily returning to normal. "Melanie? Why will *she* be calling me back?"

I don't like Melanie very much. She is a big-boned woman who thinks I'm a sissy because I whimper whenever she takes blood, a task she performs with the gentle touch of a prison guard.

"Is this Mr. Milligan?" asked Danielle, recognizing my real voice.

"No!" I lied. "Listen, I really need to speak to the doctor."

"Is this an emergency, Mr. Milligan?" Danielle asked impatiently.

"I am *not* Mr. Milligan! And yes, it *is* a bit of an emergency."

"Then you should hang up and dial 911 right away."

Oh, isn't that a fine idea? I imagined a scene where paramedics pull up to my house, sirens blaring. Two chiseled, terminally handsome young EMTs jump out and hurriedly wheel a gurney to my front door. Our neighbors gather outside, speculating on what could have happened to me this time. They're certain it couldn't be my wife, because she never does anything stupid.

Bob, who lives a few doors down and who I suspect runs a gambling business out of his garage, has started a pool on what might be wrong with me, and whether or not I will survive it. The early favorite seems to be "Gardening Accident," because someone recently saw me buying a weed whacker.

I let the paramedics in, and they're surprised to find me calm and pain-free. When I sheepishly explain my problem, one of them says, "Jeez, the way you sounded on the phone, we thought you had an extra nose growing out of your forehead or something."

"Yeah," says the other. "Or a four iron wedged in your backside."

And when they pack up to leave, they say, "For things like this, sir, you should just call your doctor."

Gee, thanks, fellas. I never thought of that.

But eventually, I swallowed my pride, talked to Melanie the Mangler, and then to my doctor, who agreed to write me a prescription. The worst was behind me, until I realized I still had to take my hard won Rx to the pharmacy.

There have been many important pieces of legislation enacted to insure that women have equal employment opportunities in whatever field they choose. I am all for that, but do so many of these women have to choose to become pharmacists?

Like many men who have reached grandfather age, I've become one of millions of lucky folks who now have a plastic pill container with the day of the week stenciled on each compartment. It also means that I've been trading at my local pharmacy for years, and whenever I go in there, they are professional, courteous, and prompt.

They also call me by my first name.

So of course there's no way I could take such a sensitive prescription to them. What would they think? The cream I needed for that rash last year was bad enough. But this?

So I devised a brilliant plan that would allow me to have my prescription filled with no further damage to my self-esteem. You are welcome to use it, if you dare.

First, I located a twenty-four-hour, drive-through pharmacy on the other side of town. Then I called and learned that working the midnight to 8:00 a.m. shift would be a new pharmacist named John. This fit my needs perfectly; by midnight, all my friends would have been asleep for at least four hours. And, as a bonus, I would be dealing with a male pharmacist, which would eliminate a lot of the embarrassment from the situation. As simple as that, I'd have my prescription in time for our anniversary, and no one would ever know a thing.

I tiptoed out of the house at five minutes before midnight for the twenty-five-minute trip to the pharmacy; when I arrived, there were three cars ahead of me in the drive-through lane.

John the pharmacist had a mirror by his window so he could see how many cars were waiting. When he eyed me, he reacted strangely, and seemed edgy and nervous about something. I assumed he had probably hoped for a slower evening.

A few minutes later, I was next in line. I gave a relieved sigh, knowing that before long I would have my magic pills, and my little problem would be solved. I put my head back, closed my eyes, and began making plans for our anniversary.

That's when I heard the sirens and screeching tires. Before I knew it, two uniformed police officers were leveling their service revolvers at me.

"Get out of the car, slowly," they shouted. "And we don't want to see anything in your hands!"

To show them I wasn't holding anything, I dropped my suddenly-sweaty prescription form on the seat, got out of my car and held up my hands, hoping to send them a message that they were dealing with a man who was extremely compliant, obedient, and petrified.

While one of the officers quickly patted me down, the other asked what I had tossed on the seat before I got out of the car.

"A prescription, sir," I replied. I added the "sir" even though this officer was young enough to be my child.

"A prescription?" he said with suspicion. "You expect me to believe that?"

"You can check for yourself, officer."

When he confirmed that it was indeed a prescription and his partner had determined that I was unarmed, they relaxed a bit, relatively certain that I was not a threat.

"Why are you out here getting a prescription at this hour, dressed like that?" the officer asked, pointing to my face.

It's then I realized why they were being so cautious with me. I was still wearing the ski mask I put on when I left home to ensure that no would recognize me.

I took off the mask and the officer who had patted me down turned me to face him.

"Coach Mike?" he asked, amazed.

But I didn't immediately recognize him.

"It's me . . . Steve Porter," he said with a big grin. "I was on your Little League team, remember? The White Sox?"

"Oh, yes, Steve, hi. How are you doing?" I said, recalling that Steve didn't have a whole lot of baseball talent. Back then, he couldn't catch a thing. To make up for that, he now catches old men out skulking for Viagra.

"This was the best coach I ever had," Steve told his partner, who returned my prescription form to me.

"Nice to meet you, sir," he said. "Sorry about the confusion. Go ahead and get your prescription. But lose the ski mask, okay?"

And then Steve pointed at the prescription and said, "Have a good time, Coach." He followed this with a rakish wink and thumbs up.

I nodded, thanked them for their understanding, and waved as they drove off.

When I finally got home with my hard-earned pills, I felt relatively confident that no one would ever be the wiser.

But three days later, when I was walking my dog, I happened past the Porters' house. Mr. Porter was outside, watering his lawn.

"Hi, Gus," I said.

"Oh, hey!" he called back. Then after a short pause, he added, "How's it going, Casanova?" And he laughed so hard he wet himself with his hose.

Serves him right.

So now that I had what I needed, I planned to use it judiciously.

But not when our grandchildren are visiting.

Or, as my wife says, should I so much as touch her with grandkids asleep in the next room, "Don't get any big ideas."

It makes me think of a book I gave my mother many years ago when our first child was born. I believe it was called *Grandmothers Are to Love*. Well, around my house, we have an updated version. It's called *Grandmothers Are to Love, Except by Grandfathers When the Grandchildren Are Around*.

FOURTEEN

THE EYE OF THE BEHOLDER

As a grandfather, I will tell anyone who will listen that I have the cutest, smartest, and most talented grandchildren ever. And those whom I can't reach personally will surely get the message from my numerous bumper stickers or the "World's Greatest Grandpa" T-shirt I get every Father's Day.

I'm sure that you feel the same way about your grandchildren; and although you know that they are all things beautiful and wonderful, there will be a few hard-to-please folks who won't be as enthusiastic about them as you are.

I've found that people like this are not discerning; they are not visionaries; they are not appreciative of childhood genius.

And they are not grandparents.

As hard as it might be for you to understand, people of this type also may not appreciate the unbelievably delightful and always-riveting stories you love to tell about your grandkids.

None of this is to suggest that any of us will stop boasting about our grandkids. But—like eating onions at lunch time—bragging should be done at your own risk. If not, you may find your friends walking away from you whenever you open your mouth.

Consider the case of Steve and Eve Reeve and Larry and Mary Carey. (I changed their names to protect both our

friendships and the $35 "Steve" still owes me from a poker game.) These four long-time friends made a date to visit a Monet exhibition at their local museum and have dinner afterward. In addition to their interest in art, Steve and Eve and Larry and Mary have almost everything in common, except for one small but significant thing: Larry and Mary have a three-year-old grandson, Jerry. Steve and Eve have no grandchildren, although they do have a grown daughter who has a live-in boyfriend, a tortoise, and two iguanas she calls her "kids."

When the foursome met in front of the museum and started up the granite steps, Larry and Mary couldn't resist telling Steve and Eve about the previous weekend, when little Jerry had stayed with them.

"He is sooo darling," Mary said.

"And very mature for his age," added Larry, as they entered the high-ceilinged foyer, "Little Jerry is almost completely potty trained! Oh, sure, he has a little accident every now and then, but never with poop-poop, only with pee-pee," he crowed. His words bounced off the elegant marble colonnades as though he were using a bullhorn.

Then Mary told Steve and Eve that "Little Jerry already knows all his colors!" as they entered the main exhibition hall.

"And not just the primaries," Larry continued. "Hues and earth tones, too."

As they approached Monet's *Rouen Cathedral in Full Sunlight*, Steve uttered, "Amazing."

Thinking that Steve's "amazing" was referring to little Jerry, Larry agreed wholeheartedly. "Yes, he *is* amazing. His pre-school teacher says most kids don't grasp all that until they're five."

"I was talking about Monet's perspective of the cathedral."

"Oh, yes, it's lovely," Mary said quickly without really studying it. "And speaking of cathedrals, we took Jerry to church with us Sunday morning. We gave him a dollar to put in the collection, but when the basket got to us, he looked inside and said, 'Look, more money!' and grabbed a handful of bills."

Larry continued with a chuckle. "And when the usher tried to take the money back from him, Jerry started screaming 'My money! My money!' It was so cute!"

Steve and Eve looked at each other and wondered who these people were and what did they do with the real Larry and Mary?

Then Eve tried to get everyone to focus on the reason they were there: Monet's timeless works of art.

"Oh, my gosh," Eve gasped, staring at the painting of the cathedral. "Look at his use of yellow."

"And *dode*," said Larry, smiling to Mary in some secret grandparent code.

"*Dode*? What the hell's *dode*?" asked Steve.

"That's how Jerry says *gold*," explained Mary. "We were going to correct him, but it's so darn precious . . ."

When they moved on to Monet's famous depictions of water lilies, Steve and Eve wondered if Precious Little Jerry would pronounce them *willies*, because that's what they were getting a case of.

Gazing at one of Monet's most famous works, *Water Lilies and Clouds*, they were all taken by its beauty. But Larry seemed particularly moved.

"You won't believe this," he said, staring at one of the world's great works by one of its great artists, "but little Jer painted something just like that last weekend."

"Who's Jer?" asked another man who was admiring the work.

"Our grandson," explained Mary to the perfect stranger she was now addressing like a lifelong friend. "He's only three, see?" she said, pulling out her billfold and producing pictures of her artistic grandson. "He did it with his paint set. Two-dollar watercolors."

The man nodded and hurried off, looking at Steve and Eve sympathetically.

"Really, guys," Larry persisted. "I mean, it's not *exactly* the same, but if you look at it at kind of an angle . . ."

Steve and Eve stared dumbfounded as their two normally intelligent friends twisted their bodies just shy of standing on their heads to look at a perfectly beautiful picture upside down.

As they all walked toward the restaurant after the exhibit, Larry and Mary continued telling what seemed to be a never-ending collection of Adorable Little Jerry stories. Mary suggested to Larry that maybe they should start checking into art schools for him. But when Larry heard this, he thought she may be getting just a little ahead of herself. "Sure, Jerry has obvious artistic talent," Larry agreed. "But he may be an even better athlete!"

Larry then told Steve how he was tossing a Nerf football with Jerry and "the little guy has the arm of Peyton Manning!" Larry wasn't sure if major college football programs actually recruited three-year-olds, but he felt it was certainly worth investigating.

When Mary received a call on her cellular, Steve seized the opportunity to take Eve aside to whisper that he'd had it with Larry and Mary. And especially with Jerry.

Steve continued that it would only get worse at the restaurant. Whatever dish they ordered, Larry and Mary would undoubtedly tell the waiter that Jerry could have prepared it better. Perhaps Jerry will be the first three-year-old college quarterback painter to attend Le Cordon Bleu! He could even design the menu covers!

Then Steve told Eve that they needed to come up with an excuse to get out of going to dinner.

Eve understood Steve's pain. She was tired of it, too. But Larry and Mary were good friends, and she wouldn't do anything to hurt their feelings. So she told Steve that he'd just have to cowboy up; there was absolutely no way she was going to be a part of any lame plan to get out of having dinner with Larry and Mary. Steve should be ashamed of himself for even considering such a thing, she told him.

When Mary concluded her phone call, she had exciting news for everyone. Of all the luck, little Jerry and his parents were in the neighborhood and they were going to join them for dinner! How great was that?

It's at this part of the story that that you should know that Eve and Steve have always considered themselves to be above-average athletes. Eve was a nationally ranked college gymnast and skier; she continues playing competitive adult soccer and volleyball, and regularly trains in Tae Bo and yoga.

Steve gets his exercise by playing in a weekly poker game.

Because of her athleticism, Eve was limber enough to break her fall when she tripped over the curb across the street from the restaurant.

When Larry and Steve saw her go down, they rushed to her assistance, helping her to her feet.

"You okay, Eve?" Larry asked as she tried to put weight on her foot.

"Agh! I don't think so," moaned Eve, grabbing her ankle. "I think I sprained it."

"We need to get some ice on that," said Steve with great concern.

"I'm sorry," Eve told her friends. "Ruining such a nice evening . . ."

"Don't be silly," Larry said. "I'm sure the restaurant has ice."

"No!" said Eve quickly. "I need to lie down and elevate it."

"That's right," said Steve. "Elevate it. High. Very high. I'll help you to the car."

"Oh, dinner would have been so much fun," Mary said sadly.

For an instant, Eve felt bad. Until Mary added, "Little Jerry will be so disappointed."

Steve and Eve shrugged apologetically, then Steve put Eve's arm over his shoulder, grabbed her waist, and helped her limp off.

"Sorry, you guys," Eve called back over her shoulder.

"Feel better," said Larry.

As soon as they rounded the corner, Eve removed her arm from around Steve's shoulder and they hurried toward their car.

"Where should we eat?" Steve asked.

"Someplace nice. With no children's menu."

"The Oak Room's not far."

"Isn't that a little pricey?"

"Yes, it is," Steve said, patting his wallet. "But you're in luck, ma'am. You're with a guy who has a *dode* card."

As they drove to the restaurant, Steve and Eve vowed that, when they became grandparents, they'd never be like Jerry and Mary. They talked about what being a grandparent can do to a person, then these two regular church-goers mused about how thick the Bible might have been if Jesus had had grandparents . . .

While walking down a village street one day, Jesus' grandparents run into a man they know.

"Hey, did you hear about what our grandson did?" the grandfather asks the man.

"You mean with the loaves and the fishes?" the man says, eager to make a hasty exit having already heard the story countless times.

"No, we're talking about what he did *yesterday*," explains the grandmother. "He walked on water."

"Walked?" the grandfather says, topping her. "He *ran*. Fastest time ever across the Sea of Galilee. By ten minutes!"

"And not only that," the grandmother continues. "He did it carrying those twelve friends of his on his back!" Then, with a caution particular to grandmothers, she adds, "Although I gotta tell you, that Judas guy looks a little shifty to me."

Later, after Steve and Eve had arrived at the Oak Room, Steve's cell phone rang. Caller ID showed that it was Larry calling.

Steve stepped into the foyer before answering.

"Hey, Steve," said Larry. "How's Eve doing?"

"Better, I think," said Steve.

"So the ice helped?" Larry wanted to know.

Steve looked toward their table, where Eve was enjoying a margarita on the rocks.

"Definitely," he said.

Then Steve heard some commotion coming over the phone.

"Oops, gotta go," said Larry with amusement. "Little Jer spilled a full water pitcher all over the table. I'm telling you … the kid is strong!"

Later during dinner, Steve and Eve received another phone call. This time it was from their daughter, with some very exciting news.

Her iguana laid eggs.

Steve and Eve were going to be grandparents!

FIFTEEN

THE BEAUTY OF BELIEF

Once you've accepted that you're actually old enough to be a grandfather, it's normal to feel proud about your little accomplishments, like leaving the house three consecutive days without forgetting to zip your pants. But if you are still not entirely comfortable with your new status, I should mention an additional bonus that goes with the position.

Unlike your *children*, who wouldn't believe a thing you told them—and probably won't until they've experienced years of parenthood for themselves—your *grandchildren* will accept as gospel truth everything their grandfather says. And not only will they believe everything you tell them— no matter how ridiculous—they will also remember it. And they will remember it far longer than you will.

To support this theory, I offer two true stories from my own life. The first I experienced as a seven-year-old grandson. The second occurred when I had been a grandfather for seven years.

1. The distance from Los Angeles to Las Vegas is approximately 300 miles, and in 1954, the drive took a little over six hours in my parents' 1949 Buick Special. I was seven years old the first time I was allowed to go along to Vegas with them and my grandparents on what would be a weekend of gambling for them and non-stop swimming for me,

supervised by my grandmother. I had just finished second grade, where I discovered that reading came very easily to me, even the big words. Of course, I didn't choose to waste this talent on things like textbooks or encyclopedias, so on this trip I decided to read every road sign along the way. And I wouldn't just read them quietly to myself; I'd announce them to my parents and grandparents so they could also enjoy my special gift of incredible literacy. It would be a spelling bee on wheels!

"Motel Next Exit!" I bellowed, as though I was heralding the arrival of the queen at Buckingham Palace.

And less than a minute later, when I shouted "Barstow, 11 Miles," I suspected that I might have a future as a railroad conductor.

After about four hours of this, my father strongly suggested that I take a nap. I told him I wasn't tired, and spotted another sign up ahead.

"Next Gas, 42 Miles," I screeched, looking at my mother for approval. Instead, she closed her eyes and began massaging her temples. I assumed her headache was caused by my father, who insisted on driving with opened windows instead of using the air conditioner, worried that the car would overheat in the middle of the desert.

When I spotted an approaching series of Burma Shave signs, my father turned up the AM radio to a Bing Crosby song. My grandparents sat in the back, smiling, which I took as a mark of their appreciation for their oldest grandson's spectacular reading talent.

After two days of swimming in an over-chlorinated pool and catching a painful case of red-eye, it was time to head home again. I made sure I got plenty of rest before we hit the road, as there was no telling how many signs would need reading on the return trip.

But much to my disappointment, the signs on the way home were no more than mirror images of those on the first leg of our trip. Oh, I still read each one at the top of my voice; but the sense of newness, of challenge, was gone.

But then I saw a sign that I hadn't seen on the way to Las Vegas. And it had a big word on it . . . so I sounded it out in my head before I went public with it.

"In-speck–shun Stay-shun," I said. "Three Miles Ahead."

"That's right," said my grandfather. "Good reading."

"Thanks," I said. "But what do they inspect at the inspection station?"

Because it was my first trip, I didn't know that everyone driving from Las Vegas to Los Angeles is required to stop at an agricultural inspection station run by the State of California. Its mission is to prohibit plants, fruits, or shrubs that might bear insects from entering California from out-of-state. This inspection station still exists today, and if you have such a plant in your car, it will be politely confiscated by an agent of the California Department of Agriculture, who wears a uniform similar to that of a state trooper, complete with shiny badge and stiff, broad-brimmed hat.

"They inspect your ears," my grandfather told me.

"My ears? Why would anyone want to inspect my ears?" I asked, not catching the amused reactions of the others in the car.

"Because," my grandfather said with great seriousness, "they want to make sure you're not bringing back any dirt in your ears from Las Vegas. Las Vegas has dirt that's very . . . dirty."

"Really?"

"Yessirree, Bob," Grandpa said. "I hope your ears are clean. Wouldn't want them to have to keep you there."

"Keep me?" I gulped.

"Yeah. Anyone whose ears aren't clean they make stay there and wash with special California ear cleaner. Then when they get enough of 'em, they put 'em on a bus and send 'em home."

"You mean someone with dirty ears has to stay out here? Overnight?"

"Overnight? Judas Priest, it could be a week before they get enough folks to fill the bus."

Grandpa said something else, but I couldn't hear him because I was busy scrubbing my ears with some saliva that I had deposited on the tail of my T-shirt, using it as a wash-cloth. And by the time we pulled into the inspection station, my ears were redder than if I'd gone ten rounds with Floyd Patterson.

As the inspector approached our car, my father got out and spoke to him for a moment. Then they went to the back of the car and opened the trunk. I didn't dare turn around to look; I was sitting between my grandparents, ramrod straight in my seat, hoping and praying that the inspector would think I was a statue whose ears didn't need checking.

When the trunk closed, the inspector began walking around the car and—without a word—he looked into my mother's ears, then my grandmother's, and finally my grandfather's. Apparently their ears all passed muster.

Then he motioned to me. "Okay, young man, step out of the car, please."

What? Why me? My ears couldn't be as dirty as every-one else's. I remembered that no more than a month before, I'd seen my grandma Q-tip out a chunk of earwax the size of a Hanukkah candle.

As I climbed over my grandfather and stood on the swel-tering pavement, the inspector removed a small pocket flashlight and checked my right ear.

"Mmm, mmm . . ." was all he said. I took that as a bad sign. My ear probably had more wax than a beehive.

Then he shone his flashlight into my left ear.

"Oh, boy . . ." he muttered. Hearing this, I looked around to see where I'd be sleeping and wondered if coyotes and wolves would attack boys with dirty ears.

He stuck his flashlight back in his pocket and stared at me, deciding how to break the bad news.

But before he could speak, I heard my grandfather's voice.

"Officer, I'm the boy's grandfather and a veteran of the Spanish-American War," he said, getting out of the car. "First Boatswain's Mate, Pacific Fleet, Battle of Manila Bay," he explained, flashing his Navy tattoo of a dragon with an anchor in its mouth. "I know his ears are probably below standards, but he's a fine young man and an excellent reader, and I'd consider it a favor—one military man to another—if you'd let him come home with us today."

The inspector considered this for what seemed to be an hour, then looked to my grandfather. "It's a pleasure to meet you, sir," said the inspector. "And I'd be honored to do a favor for such a patriot as yourself."

I finally took a breath. The inspector crouched so he could speak to me face to face, ear to ear.

"You've got a fine grandfather, son. Now go on home and keep those ears clean."

"Yessir!" I said gratefully.

I had always loved my grandfather immensely, but never more than at that moment.

I climbed back into the car and we drove off into the sunset. I don't remember if I read any more signs the rest of the way. But I do remember promising myself that I would never drive from Las Vegas to Los Angeles again. And if I ever *had* to do it, I would leave my ears at home.

Nine summers later, when I wise old teenager of sixteen, my friend, Floyd, returned from a three-week vacation with his parents touring the West in a motor home. We sat at our kitchen table as Floyd told me about his travels while my mother washed breakfast dishes at the sink. Floyd didn't enjoy the trip at all, feeling that three weeks is entirely too long to spend with your parents; but he admitted that he did have fun when they stopped in Las Vegas on the way home. My still-red ears perked up when I heard this.

"Las Vegas? You *drove* home from Las Vegas?" I asked.

Floyd nodded, puzzled by my agitation.

"Did they check your ears?" I demanded.

Floyd didn't know what to make of my idiotic question. It was as if he had just told me he had won a million dollars and I answered him with, "Did you order the pot roast, Mrs. Hastings?"

At the sink, my mother started coughing and her shoulders began shaking. From behind, it seemed she was having some type of spasm.

"You okay, Mom?"

For some reason, my mother wasn't able to speak. But she did nod her head and hold up her hand, letting me know she was okay. Why she couldn't look at me, I had no idea.

Meanwhile, Floyd was still trying to make some sense of my question. "My ears? What the hell are you talking about?"

"When you drive home from Vegas, they check your ears for dirt," I explained. Then, as Floyd stared at me blankly, I suspected that maybe his ears were so dirty that his parents hid him under a bed in their rented motor home to avoid detection.

"There's this mean-looking police guy in a big hat, and . . ."

"Michael, could I speak to you for a moment please?" my mother asked, as she turned to me and wiped her eyes.

"*Michael*"? This must be something serious. She probably wanted to tell me she didn't approve of Floyd using words like *hell* in our house.

She took me into the next room and explained the truth about the inspection station. She would have told me years ago, but she'd forgotten all about it. Apparently everyone had. Except me.

My grandfather had lied to me.

"He didn't lie," she said. "He was just having fun with you. You were always his favorite. And I'm sure he'd tell you so if he were still with us today."

After I thought about it for a minute, I couldn't help smiling. Checking my ears for dirt? In the middle of the desert? How could I have believed such a thing? And how could I have continued believing it?

Because my grandpa told me, that's why.

2. More than forty-five years later, our seven-year-old granddaughter was swimming in the pool as my friend, Ray, and I looked on.

"Buh–Buh, look!" she insisted before each belly flop off the board. And when she'd surface, she'd ask, "Was that a good one?"

"Excellent!" I told her. "Best dive I ever saw!"

And this went on for the next 229 dives over twelve minutes.

Finally, Ray called to her, "Can you do a swan dive?"

"What's that?" she asked.

Ray, wearing jeans and a long sleeve shirt, stood on the patio and demonstrated, spreading his arms wide and sticking out his chest. You need to know that Ray is also known as Big Play Ray. This is because Ray, quite simply, is a big guy. And although he has no grandchildren of his own, Ray thoroughly enjoys being around kids almost as much as they enjoy him. I think this is because Ray—as a successful working actor for over forty years—still has a healthy amount of child living within.

When my granddaughter saw Ray's detailed, over-the-top depiction of a perfect swan dive, she was awestruck.

"Were you a diver?" she asked with reverence.

Asking Big Play Ray if he was ever a diver is like asking Richard Simmons if he was ever a Green Bay Packer.

"A diver?" I repeated. "Have you ever heard of the Olympics?" I asked my granddaughter.

"You mean the ones with Mia Hamm?" she answered immediately.

"That's right. Well, Big Play Ray was an Olympic diver in 1957." Then I turned to Ray. "What was that specialty dive you were famous for?" I asked.

Seeing that he had a rapt audience in my granddaughter, Ray the Actor took over to create Ray the Olympic Diver. "Aw, I really don't like to brag about it, but it was a triple three-and-a-half corkscrew with two twists and a flying kayah!" he said modestly.

And then, with his trademark perfect timing, he whirled and contorted to demonstrate his signature dive, and then sat down to let my granddaughter absorb it. She stared at him admiringly for a moment, and then went back to her belly flops. And that was that.

But as it turned out, that wasn't even close to that.

Four years later, this same wonderful granddaughter was now in fifth grade. One night our phone rang and I answered.

"Hi, Buh-Buh," she said.

"Hey, darlin'. How are you?"

"Okay, I guess. I have to write a paper on the most famous person I know."

Wow, what flattery. There's no better feeling than being famous in your grandchild's eyes. Because if you're famous in your *children*'s eyes, it can be very expensive.

"Sure, honey, what do you want to know?"

"Your friend Big Play Ray's phone number," she said. "I'll be the only one in my class who knows a man who dove in the Olympics. Even if he is old."

"Ray?" I stammered? "The Olympics?" What was she talking about?

"Yes. Remember when I was swimming at your house and you told me about his special dive? A kayak or something?"

Then it hit me. What had I done? For a moment, I saw my beautiful granddaughter standing in the desert with a flashlight in her ear.

"Oh, right, the kayak . . . Listen, honey, about Ray . . ." I quickly ran through a number of explanations in my head: "Ray can't talk; he lost his voice." "Ray's phone is broken." "Ray doesn't have a phone since he moved into a teepee." But I knew that would only make things worse.

"Maybe you could think of someone else to write about," I suggested.

"Like who?"

"Well . . . like me."

"Buh–Buh, you're not famous. You're a writer." Hearing her thoughts on writers, I had a horrible thought: could my granddaughter grow up to be a Hollywood producer?

"Now can I please have Ray's phone number?"

The truth would be hard, but I knew what I had to do.

"Honey, about Ray . . . He never . . ."

That's when I heard her "call waiting" beep.

"Hold on, Buh-Buh," she said.

As I waited, I hoped that someday she'd find it in her heart to trust her grandpa again.

She came back on the line. "Never mind, Buh-Buh," she said.

"Pardon?"

"Big Play Ray. I don't need to talk to him anymore."

"Why not?"

"There was a man on the news tonight and his pig had babies. And one of the baby pigs has two heads!"

"And?" I asked.

"And my friend Ashley. That's her Uncle Leroy! And she doesn't go to my school, so I'm going to write about him!"

"Wow," I said with no small mount of relief. "That's a great idea."

"Yeah. What were you going to tell me about Ray?"

"Pardon?"

"You said, 'Ray never . . .' Ray never what?"

"Oh, that. Ray never . . . Ray never is home at this time anyhow. He's out giving diving lessons."

"Oh. Well, bye, Buh-Buh. I love you."

"Love you too, sweetie. Bye."

And that night before I went to sleep, I kissed Jill good-night.

Then I thanked the Lord for friends like Ray and two-headed pigs.

SIXTEEN

THE FIVE COMMANDMENTS FOR GRANDFATHERS

Actually, there are *Ten* Commandments for grandfathers, but we'll only discuss the most important five, because now that you're of grandfather age, the last thing you need is more stuff to keep track of. Like me, I'm sure your mind is already fully occupied trying to remember things like which of those two numbers represents your *good* cholesterol, your bank-assigned PIN number, and where you parked your car at the mall.

This last example requires that I tell you a story before continuing with the Commandments. This story is true, and is one I've never told before. So if you promise not to relay it to my wife, this is a perfect time to get it off my sagging, grey-haired chest.

One day not long ago, I came out of the mall to discover that my car was not where I remembered parking it. After searching the parking structure for over an hour and still finding no trace of it, I finally had to accept the sad probability that my beloved BMW had been stolen. I called the police, who arrived quickly and began taking a crime report. As the officer transcribed my information onto a form, she asked if I happened to know the car's Vehicle Identification Number. When I told her that I could

barely remember the license number, she asked for my key ring—explaining that some manufacturers also engrave the VIN on the ignition key. When I handed her my keys, she studied them closely. Then she did something puzzling. She shot me a pitiful look and began shaking her head. I asked if there was a problem and, as politely as she could, she pointed out that the ignition key did not read "BMW." Instead, it read "JEEP." Examining the key, I felt my face grow flushed with embarrassment as I suddenly remembered one important piece of the puzzle. Jill had swapped cars with me that morning, saying that the BMW would be more comfortable for her to drive "the girls" to lunch in. I had driven her car to the mall.

I apologized to the officer for wasting her time and she left without giving me a lecture. She probably figured that no matter what she told me, I'd forget by the time I got home.

There was a silver lining, though. After the officer left, I turned to see Jill's white Jeep parked a mere two rows away. So I suppose one could argue that—subconsciously at least—I did not forget where I parked my car. I just forgot what car it was that I parked.

Now, let's get back to the Grandfatherhood Commandments. Though there is no fine or jail time for disobeying them, you should be aware that a violation can result in the revocation of your AARP benefits card.

I. THOU SHALT REMEMBER THINE AGE

What grandchildren expect from a grandfather is his undying love, his tender guidance, and his frequent disbursements of cash. What they don't want is someone who will ridicule their musical choices, urge them to do better in sports, and generally meddle in their lives.

For that, they have parents.

And, of course, their other grandfathers.

And although it's difficult for us accept the limitations of age, accept them we must. Do not be fooled by your deluded grandfather friend who proclaims that "Having a grandchild makes me feel young again!" If he feels so darned young, why does he need electric hedge clippers to trim his toenails?

The truth is that you are not young, and pretending that you are can have dire consequences. For example, let's say you have a twelve-year-old grandson who is a star baseball player. One day while you are visiting, he hands you a padded mitt and asks if you would catch him while he practices his pitching. He specifically asks *you* because you've told him of your baseball exploits when you were his age and, as we've already seen, grandchildren believe everything their grandfathers tell them.

It is now that you wish you hadn't embellished your athletic achievements. Although you *did* play baseball when you were a boy, the truth is that you spent most of your spare time in accordion lessons and collecting stamps, and were certainly not the All-Star you claimed to be. In fact, you played only two years—when you were six and seven—because your parents thought it would be a positive experience. And to say you "weren't very good" is like saying Billy Barty "wasn't very tall."

In fact, the only positive experience of your short baseball career was that both years, you had the same nice coach who gave every player a trophy designated especially for him at the end of each season. Your first year, your coach named you the team's "Most Valuable Listener." Your second and final year, you were rewarded as the "Most Improved Foul Ball Retriever."

But although your hands-on baseball experience is limited, you know enough to realize that your grandson is very talented, because you've been to a few of his games and have seen that he throws the ball hard. Very hard.

It's now that you have a difficult decision to make. If you choose to nurture your deluded self-image and perpetuate your hollow boasts, you will have to catch your grandson. And even though you recently had LASIK surgery, you know that your eyes are not keen enough to catch a ball coming at you as fast as your grandson can throw it. After all, when your wife gently lobbed you the car keys last week, they caromed off your forehead.

And since your grandson mentioned nothing about a catcher's mask, you need to calculate the price of protecting your ego versus the cost of replacing the bridgework you're still paying for.

And because he's only twelve, your grandson probably doesn't have pinpoint control. You've never owned a protective cup before, so you must also decide whether you want to risk experiencing the same breathtaking pain you endured immediately after your double-hernia surgery.

"You know what, Chuck, that's not going to work," you say.

"Why not, Poppo?" he asks.

"Well, because I'm too old. My eyes aren't that great and my reflexes are shot. Plus I never was really very good at baseball when I was a kid. In fact, I stunk."

"But you said . . ."

"I know what I said. But I only told you that to impress you. Sorry."

What are you saying?! The only way you could make a confession like that would be if you were on your death bed. So you force a smile, take the mitt, and suspect that pretty soon you will be.

II. THOU SHALT NOT COMPETE WITH THE OTHER GRANDPAS

Although it's only natural for you to want to be your grandchild's favorite, you are forbidden to use dirty tricks to gain unfair advantage. Although this Commandment is general in scope, grandfatherhood scholars have cited several specifics that are forbidden.

a) Off-handedly referring to your grandchild's other grandfather(s) in unflattering terms like "Grandpa Nose Wart," "Grandpa Out of a Job Again," or "Grandpa Rehab."

b) Purposely excluding the other grandpas from family events. For example, it is unacceptable to host a "spontaneous" barbecue to celebrate your grandson's first time wearing "big-boy pants" without inviting your counterpart and then telling your grandson, "Your other grandpa would have been here, but it was out of range for the electronic monitoring device he has to wear ever since he . . . Oh, never mind."

c) Trying to make the other grandpa's assets seem like liabilities, in spite of him being a handsome, self-made millionaire with a fleet of private jets and homes in New York, London, and Tahiti. And even though he donated his most recent seven-figure bonus to a charity he let *you* select, and spends his weekends with his seven children and wife of thirty-six years building homes for the needy, you should not try to discredit him. And just because he has recently become one of the most popular male underwear models in the world while being two years older than you, it does not entitle you to . . . Aw, hell, *these* Commandments aren't written in stone! Torpedo the pretty boy!

III. THOU SHALT ADORN THY WAIST WITH NOTHING OTHER THAN A BELT

This is universal in nature and has no exceptions, regardless of race, creed or level of fitness. And while the reason for this Commandment should be obvious to any grandfather-aged man, there are an overwhelming number of you out there who insist on breaking the Third Commandment. I know this because I have seen you.

Simply stated, this Commandment prohibits older men from going out in public wearing what is known as a "fanny pack." There are numerous reasons for this, but we only need discuss a few.

First, to wear a fanny pack, one must still own a fanny. And because most grandfathers' fannies disappeared years ago, a fanny pack will draw attention to this loss, thus making the matching shorts/shirt ensemble that your wife bought you look even goofier than it already does.

"Look at that old man wearing a fanny pack," a younger person might say to her friend as they're caught in the logjam you've created by trundling your way down the middle of the sidewalk on a balmy, sunny day.

"I see," says her friend. "I wonder what's holding it up in back? The man has absolutely no fanny!"

"You're right about that," says the first girl with a sympathetic giggle. "No, wait, I think I see it!" she says as they hop through some ivy to pass you. "I believe his fanny has moved from his rear to his front!"

Fanny packs are perfectly acceptable for young people who roller skate, for old women who collect things, and for tourists from Eastern Europe and Ohio. If you're in none of these categories, here is a way for you to determine whether you should wear one of these annoying accoutrements: If your navel used to point due west but now points south or southwest, lose the fanny pack.

Going "packless" should not be at all difficult, since you have already spent most of your life not wearing one. If pockets were good enough for over fifty years, what makes you think you suddenly need a fanny pack? In reality, the older you get, the fewer things you need to carry with you. No business cards or appointment calendars; and because you no longer get job performance bonuses, your wallet is now a lot thinner and fits into your rear pants without hurting your fanny, even if you still had one.

The final reason grandfathers are forbidden to wear fanny packs is perhaps the most important: As men get older, they become more forgetful. This can result in a grandfather going to a restaurant with his fanny pack, removing it while he eats, then forgetfully leaving it behind. Last year, in fact, there were over five thousand reported cases of absent-minded older men leaving restaurants without their fanny packs—and their wallets. But the number of lost wallets is significantly smaller for men who choose to keep them in their trouser pockets. In fact, over the past two years, there was only *one* report of a grandpa leaving an establishment without his pants. And that was because of an incident involving his grandson's bachelor party.

In addition to fanny packs, this Commandment also prohibits older men from wearing one of those mesh waistband devices for holding bottled water. At your age, you have enough trouble holding the water you already have in you, so why tempt fate by drinking more?

Note that this Commandment does not apply to tool belts for those of you who are professional tradesmen, artisans, or craftsmen. Because if you are any of these, your grandchildren are likely very proud of you and will invite you to speak at their school to tell their class about all the wonderful things you've built.

If, however, you are a recently-retired insurance salesman and your entire tool collection consists of a hammer, two screwdrivers, and a can of WD-40, you are not allowed to wear a tool belt—or even buy one—even though you have plenty of time on your hands and just graduated at the top of your class from a two-day Home Depot course on "How to Add a Second Story to Your Home."

There is also a corollary to this Commandment which prohibits a grandfather from wearing his baseball cap backwards unless, at the age of sixty-seven, he is still a full-time major league catcher.

IV. THOU SHALT NOT SHOW FAVORITISM

Although it goes without saying that you love every one of your grandchildren, you need to understand the difference between the words "love" and "prefer." For example, while you may *love* steak, you may *prefer* a rib-eye. This is not to diminish your deep feelings for the T-bone, the New York strip, or even the flank steak. You truly care for all of them, and would defend them against anyone who said anything bad about them, including your mortician.

The same applies to your grandchildren. You *love* them all unconditionally, but you *prefer* the six-year-old granddaughter who tells you that she wants to marry a handsome, funny, smart man just like you. She is your Rib-Eye, while your fourteen-year-old grandson who never speaks and tromps around the mall with his baggy pants belted three inches above his knees is your Flank Steak.

But while your love for all your grandchildren is permanent, it is not unusual for your preferences to vary. This change usually results from events that come at you without warning—like your fourteen-year-old, non-speaking, underwear-showing Flank Steak calling you out of the blue and asking if you could teach him how to play cribbage.

When he arrives the next day, you wonder how he is able to walk with his pants like that. His low belt makes him take short, quick steps, which would be fine if he were in training to become a geisha. You also wonder what brought on his sudden interest in cribbage, a card game that's not at all popular among young people, and one that you learned from your grandfather.

When you ask him, he reminds you about his volunteer work at a senior home that's part of his high school curriculum.

"I thought you were only required to do that last semester," you say.

"Uh-huh," he mumbles, then explains, "I'm kinda doin' it on my own this semester."

"You mean for no credit?"

"Yeah. See, there's this old guy, George, who lives there. No one ever visits him, and he likes to play cribbage, so I figured I'd learn how."

"I'd say George is a lucky man."

"He's a cool old dude. You know . . . Like you, Grandpa."

And that's how a Flank Steak becomes a Rib-Eye.

So there's really no way to avoid having a favorite, even though that favorite may change from time to time.

The trick—as the Fifth Commandment ordains—is to avoid showing it. You must treat every grandchild with the same amount of love and respect.

And if you think this is easy, talk to the grandparents of Jimmy and Billy Carter.

Or Bill and Roger Clinton.

Or the Baldwin Brothers.

Rib-Eyes and Flank Steaks.

V. THOU SHALT KNOW WHEN TO ZIP THY LIP

Today's young parents do things a lot differently than we did, and I often wonder if the part of the brain that governs common sense is somehow adversely affected by those who consume too many four-dollar lattes. For instance, many of today's parents actually believe they should try to *reason* with a three-year-old.

Consider:

2008: "I don't see why I have to go to bed now," the toddler shouts. "Give me one good reason!"

"Okay, sweetie, let's discuss it."

1980: "I don't see why I have to go to bed now! Give me one good reason!"

"Okay, sweetie. The reason is 'cause I said so! Nighty-night!"

But a grandfather needs to refrain from commenting on his children's parenting practices unless he's asked, which will never happen because our children think they have found the true path to proper parenting.

Just like we did.

But holding your tongue is not always easy. Imagine that you call your six-year-old grandson to find out what he'd like for his upcoming birthday. Your daughter answers.

"Hi, honey," you say. "Is little Roscoe home?"

"No, Daddy. He's at a play date."

"A what?"

"A play date," she repeats.

"What the hell's that?" you ask.

"He made a date to go play with his friend Barlow."

"Barlow? Isn't that the kid who lives right next door?"

"That's right."

"Are you telling me that Roscoe had to make a date just to go next door?"

"Daddy . . ." she says, sensing that you may be having trouble with this parenting concept.

What you want to say next is, "*Play date*? Are you kidding me? Why does he have to make a date to play? What happened to running next door and yelling, 'Hey, Barlow, wanna play?' Or is Barlow too busy heading up a multi-national corporation to be allowed to play without an appointment?" A play date! Who comes up with this stuff? You've never heard such a crock! What does your daughter call dinner at her house? A nourishment date?

But instead, you must use the wisdom of your age to bite your tongue.

"That's nice," you say sweetly. "Could you please have Roscoe call me when he gets home from his play date?"

"Sure, Daddy. He'll be back in an hour."

But two hours later, Roscoe still hasn't called, so you call him again. This time your son-in-law answers.

"Oh, hi, Jim," he says to you. "What's up?"

"Same ol', same ol'. Can I talk to Roscoe for a sec?"

"Uh, hold on," your son-in-law says uneasily. Then he covers the phone and you can tell he's having an exchange with your daughter. Finally, he comes back on the line.

"He, uh, he can't talk to you right now, Jim."

"Oh, I'm sorry. Are you eating dinner?"

"No. Roscoe's having a time-out."

"A time-out?" you ask.

"Yep," says your son-in-law.

"A time-out? You mean he was playing basketball or something?"

"No, Jim. Roscoe's having a *time-out*." This time, he says the word slowly, thinking that he may be talking too fast for someone your age.

"A time-out from what?"

"From everything. After he came home from his play date, he was a little too rambunctious, so Colleen gave him a time-out."

"You mean she sent him to his room?"

"No, to the living room sofa."

"Roscoe's on your living room sofa?"

"Uh-huh."

"Doing what?"

"Sitting."

"Just sitting?"

"That's right. That's what time-outs are for."

"For sitting?"

"And for thinking about what he did wrong and realizing that he's responsible for his actions, and that those actions have consequences."

"A six-year-old will get all that from sitting? Couldn't he read a book or something?"

"No, that would be rewarding him."

You realize that if you continue biting your tongue at this rate, it will have more holes in it than Phil Spector's alibi.

But again, you must take the high road.

"Okay," you sigh. And then you schedule a *phone date* with Roscoe just as soon as he finishes his time-out.

And don't think that your child's approach to parenting only evidences itself *after* the child is born.

Our friends Charlie and Cynthia got their first hint of today's New Age parenting several months before they became grandparents. Their daughter, Janice, was in the seventh month of her first pregnancy, and they were attending a baby shower for her in Northern California. Although Charlie has had a long and successful career as a television comedy writer, he's learned that telling people what he does for a living can sometimes be a mistake. Some will either respond with, "God, how can you write that stuff? Whatever happened to shows like *All in the Family*?" Others will say, "Comedy writer, eh? My Uncle Bert works at the DMV, and he has so many funny stories. I'll give him your number!"

"So, Mr. Smith," said the short, plump, plain-looking woman as she approached Charlie at the backyard shower. "Janice tells me you're a writer," she said with admiration.

Charlie nodded politely. At least his daughter still thought what he did was kind of cool.

"What do you write?"

"Television," he answered.

The disappointment in her eyes was immediate and profound. "Oh, I don't watch television," she sniffed. "Unless it's PBS, of course."

"Of course," Charlie sighed. Then he asked what she did for a living.

"I'm a doula," she said.

"A what?" Charlie blurted. Was she admitting to being a member of some kind of sleeper cell? He scanned her belt for explosives. She looked clean, although on closer inspection, Charlie thought he detected just a trace of a dark stubble.

"Doula. Three of us will be assisting Janice at childbirth to provide a tranquil and peaceful environment for her newborn to arrive and thrive."

It took Charlie a while to process this. His daughter ran a successful consulting company all by herself, yet she needed three women to help her have a baby? She already had an OB/GYN and pediatrician that she raved about, plus she and her husband had been attending birthing classes twice a week for over two months. Why did she need these women? What would they do? Wave pom-poms and cheer, "Go, Janice! Go Janice!"?

"You mean you're a midwife?" Charlie asked the woman.

When the young lady heard that, Charlie could tell he'd made a huge gaffe. It was as if he had just met Wolfgang Puck and said, "Oh, you're a fry cook." The pudgy doula nearly leapt out of her Birkenstocks and strangled him.

"Don't you know anything about having a baby these days?" she asked with clenched jaw.

"Not much," Charlie said. "Just what I see on PBS."

A few minutes later, when his wife came over to join him, Charlie was still flabbergasted. "Cynth, do you know that when Janice has her baby, she's gonna . . ."

"The doulas, right?" Cynthia asked, rolling her eyes. "I just heard."

"What is she thinking? When she was born, it was you and her doctors in there with her. She needs three women?"

"I don't get it, either," Cynthia said. "Janice said all her friends are using doulas these days. It's kind of a fad or something."

"Hula Hoops are a fad! Nehru jackets are a fad! Needing three midwives to have a baby isn't a fad. It's nuts!"

"Doulas," Cynthia corrected with an ironic smile.

"Okay, fine. Since you're so up on the subject, can you tell me the difference between a midwife and a doula?"

Cynthia thought about this for a moment, then said, "About fifty dollars an hour."

Charlie never said a word to his daughter about it, though. Even when he later overheard the non-television-watching doula in a heated discussion with her boyfriend—a Chinese herbalist who should know better than to wear a ponytail—about who would be the next person thrown off *Survivor.*

SEVENTEEN

WORKIN' THE PERKS

Not only is grandfatherhood wonderfully rewarding on a personal and emotional level, but you will discover that it also provides a number of benefits that you should take advantage of every chance you get. And as you gain experience as a grandfather you will undoubtedly discover more perks designed especially for you, but here are a couple of my favorites to get you started.

American Idle

Psychologists have long held that the act of singing can help relieve stress, ease tension, and cause you to make a fool of yourself in karaoke bars. What's more, one recent television commercial claims that frequent singing can add up to four years to your life. And when I heard a companion spot suggesting that everyday laughter can expand your life by up to *eight* years, I determined that if we all walked around singing "Weird Al" Yankovic songs, we could prolong our lives by *twelve* years! But we would probably not have many friends.

But whatever the numbers, it's universally agreed that singing is a healthy thing. However, a grandfather should be cautioned that—if he's in a public place and not accompanied by his grandchildren—he should not break into a

raucous rendition of "Louie, Louie" or any other song from his youth.

Let's say you're in line at the grocery store when an instrumental version of one of your favorite oldies begins playing in the background.

At first, you don't really pay attention because you're too busy trying to make sense of the stack of coupons your wife made you take before she allowed you leave the house. But as you check to make sure you have the right coupon for a $.75 discount on a 400-pound bag of sugar, you become subliminally aware of the music and, without really knowing it, begin singing along. Soon, you are disturbing people as far away as the produce section.

"*Monday, Monday,*" you sing. "*So good to me. Monday morning, it was all I hoped it would be.*" You think you're sounding so good that you wonder why Mama Cass didn't ask you to be the third Papa. "*Oh, Monday morning, Monday morning couldn't guarantee that Monday evening you would still be here with me. Monday, Monday . . .*"

Then you hear the twenty-two-year-old clerk clear her throat, and you look up to see you're holding up the line, and that people are glaring at you impatiently and wondering why the older man in the *Grandpa Rocks* sweatshirt is singing so loud.

It's then that you're hit with a hard lesson: If you're young and sing in line, people smile and tap their feet. But if you're older, they raise their eyebrows sympathetically, particularly if you forget the lyrics and have a bottle of wine in your shopping cart.

Those people don't understand that even though a man may be older, he still has plenty to sing about. Maybe he's happy because his blood pressure medication came off patent and went generic. Or maybe the forty-five-year-old suck-up who took his job just got canned for having some strange pictures on his laptop. Or perhaps he found out that Sansabelt pants are making a comeback.

But whatever the reason for your singing, people are still likely to see you as nothing but a doddering old coot.

But if you're singing along to the market's muzak while holding your three-year-old granddaughter, people will no longer see you as an old man who likely wears his undershorts backwards and inside out. Instead, they will look at you with admiring smiles. Some of the women in line may even sigh.

"*He's so fine, doo-lang, doo-lang, doo-lang. Wish he were mine, doo-lang, doo-lang, doo-lang, doo-lang . . .*" you croon as your granddaughter giggles, staring at you with utter enjoyment.

"Oh, look at how that beautiful little girl loves her grandfather," one woman thinks.

"And he has a very nice voice. I'll bet she grows up to be the free-spirited type. Just like him," thinks another.

And just like that, you have gone from a doddering old coot to a free-spirited Tony Bennett.

And until she's about ten, your granddaughter will occasionally ask you, "Grandpa, can you sing that *doo-lang* song again?" And out of experience, you will answer, "Sure, honey. Just as soon as we get to the supermarket."

Comfort Clothing

It's a known fact that as men get older, we dress less for style and more for comfort. I think this is why Levi-Strauss developed jeans labeled "Relaxed Fit," which in clothes-design lingo, means "Pants for geezers who love Coldstone Creamery ice cream and hot pastrami sandwiches."

And because we dress for comfort, every grandfather has a favorite "comfort combo"—an old shirt with a ragged collar, pants with a hole in both rear pockets, and penny loafers that haven't been resoled since the break-up of the Kingston Trio.

But as much as we love these outfits, our wives forbid us wear them anywhere we might be seen by other human beings. This includes taking out the trash, bringing in the morning paper, and even opening the door for the pizza delivery kid, whose idea of a nice shirt is any one that doesn't hide the tattoo on his sternum.

But one weekend when your wife is out of town visiting her sister, you're wearing your outfit and decide to go out for coffee, assuming that no one will pay any attention to what you're wearing.

But no sooner do you shuffle into your neighborhood donut shop than an older man spots you and whispers to his wife, "Look at those clothes! Isn't that Martha Ferkenberger's husband?"

You hear him quite clearly because when older people think they're whispering, they're actually speaking at a volume level that would drown out a Hoover industrial vacuum.

"Yes, it is," says his wife. "Poor Martha. I hear he hasn't been the same since he retired from the insurance company and bought a tool belt."

"And last week Jim saw him at Home Depot!" her husband tells her. "Something about adding a second story."

You pretend you didn't hear them and leave with your coffee. What you don't know is that, because of your outfit, they followed you to make sure you were able to find your way home before too many other people saw you dressed like that.

Now let's look at the same scenario, but this time, your grandchild is involved.

It's two weeks later, and your five year-old grandson is visiting. Once again, it's Saturday morning and you are wearing your comfort outfit. Your wife is out shopping with the child's mother and your credit card. They are shopping because your daughter is pregnant again, this time with a girl. They are giddy because "now we can buy some *really cute* baby clothes."

"Grandpa, do you have any donuts?" your grandson asks.

"No, Luke, I don't think we do."

But when you see his look of disappointment, you quickly say, "But I know where we can get some!"

This time, when you walk into the donut shop, no one seems to notice your outfit. Instead, all they see is your grandson holding your hand and looking up at you like you're the most wonderful human being in the world.

And when you say to the clerk, "Yessir, my grandson would like a glass of milk and two of your finest chocolate donuts, please," you hear a lady whisper to her friend. "Look at that man with his grandson. Isn't that cute?"

And her friend says, "It sure is. And look how he hurried out of the house without changing out of those old clothes, just so the little boy wouldn't have to wait for his donuts. He doesn't care how he looks. I love a man who's secure with himself."

And when your grandson finishes his donuts, he says, "Thank you, Grandpa," and gives you a big, wet, gooey, chocolaty kiss.

And those two women look at you and think, "What a wonderful grandpa!"

And you know what? They're right.

EIGHTEEN

THE GRAND(PA) FINALE

So you made it to "Grandpa." Or "Po-Po," or "Bappa," or whatever wonderfully goofy name your grandchild has lovingly bestowed on you. You've accepted that you're actually old enough to qualify for the position and hopefully you're embracing it, luxuriating in it, and looking forward to all the wonderful things that come with the title of Grandfather.

But remember that it also brings some responsibilities, especially if you are a full-time grandparent to your grandchild.

Life sometimes leads us down a road for which we have no map, and those of you who have taken your grandchildren into your home to raise and nurture deserve the utmost respect. What you are doing is a very difficult job, and probably not one you volunteered for. But your grandchildren need your guidance, love, discipline, and patience. And because you give it to them without question, you are heroes. And certainly your grandchildren know it.

★   ★   ★   ★   ★

It's important that grandfathers possess certain qualities, and I've learned from my grandchildren that one of them is what I call "pretendability."

My most recent example of this came while I was spending a quiet Sunday morning planted on my den

sofa, concentrating on the crossword puzzle, when my granddaughter Samantha approached. "All right, sir," she said to me politely. "Thank you for waiting. Jenny's ready to do your hair now."

Two questions immediately occurred to me: Who is Jenny, and what is it that she intends to do to my hair?

"Sam . . ." I said, wanting to finish the puzzle.

"Buh-Buh," she whispered sternly. "My name's not Sam; it's Heather. I own this hair place."

"Oh, I see," I said, realizing we were moving into make-believe. I also realized my crossword puzzling would have to wait.

"Well," I said to Samantha, "if you're Heather, who's Jenny?"

"My best hair stylist. She's right over there."

Samantha (Heather) pointed to her three-year-old sister, Alexandra (Jenny), who was holding a hair brush from her Dallas Cowboys Cheerleader Barbie set and a spray bottle of Windex. I could guess what she intended to do with the brush, but the Windex puzzled me. Maybe she thought my hair needed a good industrial-strength washing.

Then Samantha called her little sister over. "Okay, Jenny. He's ready!"

As Alexandra ran over and prepared to attack my head, Samantha indicated that I should get off the sofa and sit on the floor so it would be easier for Jenny to work her magic, whatever it might be.

"How do you want your hair cut today, Buh-Buh?" Alexandra asked me, not realizing that she had just broken one of the cardinal rules of pretendability. As her grandfather, it was my job to set her straight.

"Who's Buh-Buh?" I asked her. "My name's Zack."

This puzzled the three-year-old, who hadn't yet amassed the pretending experience of her older sister.

"Hello, *Zack*," Samantha jumped in with a smile. A big wink was all the explanation Alex needed.

"Oooohhh!" she said, catching on. "So, Zack, how do you want me to fix your hair?" she asked.

"I think I'll have a double dockenfeller on top, with a bi-lateral klondiker on the sides."

"Okay," she said, not giving it another thought. "I did one of those yesterday." Then she prepared to spray Windex on my hair.

"Don't worry, Zack," Samantha confided. "It's only blue water. We put a melted popsicle in there." Then she handed Alexandra a handful of rubber bands.

Seven minutes and three gallons of sticky water later, Alex finished her work of art and handed me a mirror. My head was drenched, with rubber bands knotting my hair into about 325 stiff, dripping clumps.

"What do you think?" the girls asked.

What I thought was that I looked like Buckwheat in the episode of *The Little Rascals* where Spanky and he fell into a lake. But the girls thought I looked beautiful, and rewarded me with two delightful, mushy kisses on the cheek before they ran off to play "Starbucks Lady."

This reminds me of a story. Over the years, I've had the privilege to work with a number of wonderfully talented comedians. Among my short list of favorites is an intelligent, amazingly clever young man named Carlos Oscar, the father of two young girls. He tells a story about his younger daughter who received one of those Playschool "restaurant" sets for her birthday. As she was playing one day, Carlos passed by and she informed him that her restaurant was now a Starbucks.

"Would you like to order something, sir?" she asked.

"Yes, I would," said Carlos. "I'd like a Grande Nonfat Latte."

"Okay," his daughter replied, punching some buttons on her plastic cash register. "That will be twenty-three dollars and fifty cents."

"What?" Carlos asked. "That usually costs three dollars. Why so much?"

"Because," his daughter said without batting an eye, "my Starbucks is at the airport!"

Over the years, I've also been called upon to play characters like *Shane*, a third-grade student when Sydni was six and wanted to play "Miss Summers, School Teacher," and *Cody*, a restaurant customer who Samantha had a crush on when she pretended to be a waitress named Marsha.

And while pretendability is an important quality for grandfathers, perhaps even more important is that of wisdom. You must understand that since your grandchildren see you as the oldest person on the planet, they also expect you to be the smartest.

"Grandpa, how fast could *Tyrannosaurus rex* run?" your five-year-old grandson asks after watching a dinosaur video. By the look on his face, you can tell that he chose to ask you because you were probably once chased by one.

"That's a good question," you tell him. "Mr. Rex was fast. Very fast."

"Faster than a speeding bullet?" he asks.

"Apparently not, or he'd still be around," you say. This satisfies him for now; but that night you research everything you can find on the beast. You phone your grandson the next day, ready to present all the information you've gathered. He'll be thrilled.

"Twenty-eight miles per hour," you tell him.

"Huh?" he says.

"That's how fast a *Tyrannosaurus rex* could run. Twenty-eight miles an hour."

Silence. A silence that tells you he has no idea what you're talking about, and that yesterday's conversation has gone to that mysterious place where all forgotten conversations with five-year-olds disappear.

Then he speaks. "Okay, Grandpa. Whatever. Bye." Then he drops the phone and scampers off to find his mother so maybe she can make some sense of what you were talking about.

But as your grandchildren get older, you'll find that their questions will be a bit more probing. And they still believe that you do have the answers. Or perhaps they just *want* to believe it.

Recently, my oldest granddaughter and I went out to lunch together. Sitting across from her, I found it hard to believe that—seemingly overnight—she had grown from the baby I held just after she was born into a beautiful and intelligent thirteen-year-old young lady whose days of playing "school teacher" were well behind her. When Sydni finished telling me about a boy in her class whose grandmother had just died, she thought for a moment, then asked me, "Buh-Buh, do you believe there's a heaven?"

In truth, with all the seeming madness in today's world, I sometimes wonder. But that discussion was for another day. Like when she gets her Doctorate in Philosophy.

"Yeah, I do think there is," I told her. "What about you?"

"Well, I *want* to," she said.

So I asked her what she thought heaven was like.

"Well, I think it's where you go when you die and everyone you ever loved in your whole life is there waiting for you. Even Domino." (Their family Dalmatian had gone to the Big Ranch in the Sky several months earlier.) "And I think everyone's always happy, and no one has to be homeless and there aren't any wars. And Alexandra doesn't have cystic fibrosis anymore."

"Wow," I said honestly. "That's exactly what I think heaven is like, too."

She was glad to hear this, but as she swirled her ice cream with her spoon, I sensed that there was something else she wanted to talk about. And whatever it was, she was giving it a lot of thought.

"Buh-Buh," she finally said, choosing her words carefully. "If you die before I do . . ."

"Yeah?" I asked.

"I mean, like waaaaaayyyy before I do . . ."

"Okay, Syd, I get the point," I said with a laugh.

"Okay. So, like, when I die and go to heaven, and you're already there, you'll remember me, won't you?"

Wow. So that was it.

"Sydni," I said, trying to keep my heart where it belonged, "I could never, ever forget someone as special as you."

"Oh, good," she said with a relieved sigh.

Then she offered me a bite of her strawberry sundae.

It tasted great.

And that was a very good grandfather day.

ACKNOWLEDGMENTS

Without the encouragement, advice, and mentoring of Daniel Lazar at the Writers House, this book would not exist. Thanks, Dan and Josh, for your patience and humor. Likewise, I am forever grateful to the good folks at Skyhorse, especially Mark Weinstein, for his belief in this project and for his incisive editing, done with a sharp, tasteful eye and fine humor. And for the amazing illustrations, thanks to the enormously talented Renee Reeser Zelnick.

Thank you, Mr. Bill Cosby—not only for the kindness of your words here, but for the gifts of laughter, intelligence and inspiration you continue giving people everywhere. And thanks for hiring me all those times, too.

To the extremely beautiful and beguiling Sydni, Samantha, Alexandra, and Claire for being wonderful muses and for providing an aging, goofy grandfather with the unbridled joy he needed for this project. Thanks for letting me tell people about you.

I'm particularly lucky to have a loyal squad of cheerleaders. Led by my ever-smiling Jill, they have been incredibly supportive, generous, and encouraging every step of the way. Ray and Marlene, Mady, Zip and Denise, Patti and Dave, you are the absolute best. Next round is on me. But don't hold me to that.

To Leroy and Carol, Tim and Cindy . . . thanks for sharing.

And finally, to John, Kevin, Rebecca, Ron, Dionn, Kevin, and Mischon, the parents of some wonderful grandchildren, both present and future. (Hint, hint . . . and you know who you are.)

ABOUT THE AUTHOR

Michael Milligan has been a working comedy writer for over thirty years, with credits including *Good Times, Maude, All in the Family, The Jeffersons,* and *Dear John.*

In *this* century, he's had the unique pleasure and good fortune to work with Mr. Bill Cosby on several projects, including *Here and Now* and Nickelodeon's *Fatherhood.* Series he's written have been acknowledged with Good Housekeeping's Award for Family Television, as well as awards for excellence from the NAACP, GLAAD, and the organizations Nosotros, Alma, and Imagen.

Michael lives with his wife, Jill, in Los Angeles, which is 316.5 miles and a five-hour drive from their grandchildren. Unless Jill drives, because he claims she can make it in four hours and thirty-seven minutes. And Michael tells us she has a distended bladder and two diplomas from traffic school to prove it.